S0-AGR-171

"(Gurian's) skillful characterizations, convincing dialogue and rich details make this a worthwhile, entertaining collection."

—*Publishers Weekly*

"Timely . . . a fascinating look into a world that remains impossibly foreign and opaque to most Americans."

—*Kirkus Reviews*

"Translucent stories! Courageous! While the rest of the world is gearing for war with the Muslims, Michael Gurian is calling for something higher, better, the kind of peace that only a first-rate storyteller can imagine."

—Jim Connor, author of *Silent Fire*

Central Skagit Sedro-Woolley Library
802 Ball St.
Sedro-Woolley WA 98284
Sept 2019

"We could not . . . important, true or better book about the 'politics' of . . . especially, about the truths hidden in the human soul than we find in *The Blind Woman and Other Stories*."

—Terry Trueman, Printz Honor author of *Stuck in Neutral*

"These stories immerse us in the mysteries that attract us to, and repel us from, foreign cultures. These are very important narratives for our time. In them, individuals of various ages, genders and faiths reveal how culture can save us or fail us, at times simultaneously. I saw these stories as a narrative bracelet which, once put on, cannot be turned away from. Their beauty and unsentimental power are stunning."

—Michael B. Herzog, author of *Troilus and Criseyde*

THE BLIND WOMAN
And Other Stories

Central Skagit Sedro-Woolley Library
802 Ball St.
Sedro-Woolley WA 98284
Sept 2019

Selected Previous Works

Fiction

An American Mystic
The Miracle
The Odyssey of Telemachus

Nonfiction

The Wonder of Boys
The Wonder of Girls
Boys and Girls Learn Differently
Saving Our Sons
The Minds of Girls
The Wonder of Aging
The Soul of the Child

Poetry

Emptying
The Sabbath
Ancient Wisdom, Modern Words
As the Swans Gather

the blind woman
and other stories

Michael Gurian

Latah Books
Spokane, Washington

The Blind Woman and Other Stories
Copyright © 2018 Michael Gurian

All rights reserved.
No part of this book may be used or reproduced in any manner
whatsoever without written permission except in the case of
brief quotations embodied in critical articles and reviews. For
permissions contact: editor@latahbooks.com

This book is a work of fiction. Any references to historical
events, real people, or real places are used fictitiously. Other
names, characters, places, and events are products of the
author's imagination, and any resemblance to actual events or
places or persons, living or dead, is entirely coincidental.

Cover design by Marina Gulova

ISBN: 978-0-9997075-6-2
Cataloging-in-Publication Data is available upon request

Manufactured in the United States of America

Book design and production by Gray Dog Press
www.graydogpress.com

Published by
Latah Books, Spokane, Washington
www.latahbooks.com

Previously printed and reviewed as
Making Peace with the Muslims

The author may be contacted at: michaelgurian@comcast.net

Selected Stories
1987 – 2001

For Gail, Gabrielle, and Davita

contents

the blind woman

Laurie Fuller arrived at the house in a pouring rain. She parked the car at the curb on 63rd Avenue, experiencing the mixture of sadness and anticipation that accompanied a new case. Trained as an RN at the University of Nebraska, Lincoln, she had come out to the University of Washington for hospice training. She had fallen in love with the Pacific Northwest, although she did not like the rain that was so common in Seattle.

Laurie ran toward the house with her coat raised up over her head. It was a blue house with white trim, 1960s architecture, lots of yard, with a rose bush and some perennial hydras out front. On the doorjamb was a beautiful blue-gray symbol—swirling letters in Arabic. Laurie hesitated a second at the door, which had been left open for her.

She always entered a case with the self-protective knowledge that there were universal patterns to dying. She had always felt that to care for the terminally ill at the site of death brought out the best in her. With her own parents dying when she was five, and her upbringing turned over to a kind but childless aunt and uncle, the certainty of death had been her childhood companion. She knew its griefs and its tremblings.

Laurie was twenty-five, magna cum laude, a premier soccer player, and the president of her school's National Organization for Women chapter. She prided herself on her certainty about life's most important things, and her ability to impose herself when needed. Five-foot-eight, muscular, pretty, with long brown hair, bright blue eyes, an aquiline nose, and full lips and dimples,

Laurie had once told a boyfriend, "I was deprived of my parents, so I decided not to deprive myself of anything I need or want in life." Six months later she broke up with Mark, who she sensed was becoming like most men—controlling, possessive of her time, and bent on depriving her of her independent self.

Laurie leaned forward and called through the screen door. "Mrs. Marshall?"

Thunder crashed and rumbled behind her. Soaking wet and shivering, she peered into the house which resembled her own childhood home except for the Muslim ornament.

Laurie pressed against the screen door and knocked harder, hoping to see Tess Mostabi Marshall, the woman she'd met two days before at the initial interview. Tess was the dying woman's sixty-year-old daughter, as well as her guardian. Other Mostabi children, friends, and grandchildren were due to arrive from other cities in a day or so, to join Tess as the advanced cancer finally brought death to her mother. Laurie had not met anyone in this case except Tess, had not even spoken yet with Mrs. Lila Mostabi, eighty-one, who had just been moved back home from the hospital yesterday to begin a likely three-to-five-day completion of life.

"Here I am! Call me Tess, remember." The smiling woman appeared, gray-haired, darkly pigmented (half African and half Caucasian), deep brown eyes. Her plain gingham dress was covered by an apron of tiny brown teddy bears and her hands rotated a white drop towel. She pushed the screen door open and offered her hand for shaking.

Laurie had noticed at the interview that Tess liked to shake hands a lot—not like men did, to display strength or power, but more just to touch. Laurie had been intrigued to learn from her supervisor that "some Muslims shake hands a lot." Laurie had further learned that this was a close Muslim family. The dying mother, the file reported, was from Somalia, born Lila Worku. She married a white American engineer, moved with him to Atlanta, and gave birth to their daughter, Tess, before he abandoned them. She then married an African named Deisuel Mostabi, who was a student at the university where Lila worked on the cleaning staff. Lila had become a citizen upon her first marriage, and she and Deisuel decided to remain in America. Deisuel died of a massive heart attack a decade before Lila contracted lung cancer eighteen months ago.

Curious about Islamic customs, Laurie had read Lila Mostabi's file carefully. Laurie had met some Muslims at college but spent no time with them—the men seemed the essence of patriarchy, and the women docile. Most of the Muslims she'd seen were from the Middle East. She could barely recall one from Africa.

"How is your mother doing?" Laurie asked, pulling back a hand moistened both by rain and dishwater.

"Having a good day, I think. Come in, come in. Let's see her." Tess spoke with a unique kind of southern American accent—not African American, yet not redneck either. It carried a smoothness of inflection, almost an elegance.

Tess clearly meant to be followed down a hallway. She turned, moving to a bedroom. Laurie passed a living room filled with art, mainly from Africa—a black statue of a female head with long ears (or were those long ears actually ear lobes hanging down, weighted by some black ornament?); three colorful animal masks mounted on the wall; a footstool of copper or brass, shaped like a long-bodied elephant.

"Mama?" Tess called in as they entered the first bedroom on the right.

Good, Laurie thought, *the bedroom is close to the living room.* So often, the bedroom was not large enough for the full force of dying—a custom-made bed, visitors, a television, flowers—and thus had to be moved to the living room. For Laurie, the move to the larger space was simpler with less ground to cover.

"Mama, it's Laurie, the hospice nurse."

Mrs. Mostabi had dark black skin, much darker than her daughter's complexion. She lay on her back, her eyes—in a very wrinkled, small face—staring upward at a white stucco ceiling, her hands—black on the outside, reddish on the palms—half-crooked on the edge of each hip. The large bed, which had been brought in yesterday, took up a third of the room and had an IV behind it. There was a piano, flowers, plants, and a card table with bills and other papers on it. Tess must have been doing family finances while sitting with her mother.

"Hello, Mrs. Mostabi," Laurie said as she smiled.

She knew that about two years ago, and unrelated to her cancer, Mrs. Mostabi had begun to lose her sight. Though her seemingly ancient head turned toward the new voice, and her watery brown eyes gazed at the new person, there was no sight there except the images conjured in the mind of the blind. Laurie took Mrs. Mostabi's right hand, clasping it firmly and kindly, watching the electric signs on eyelids and brow of more images forming within. Tess brushed a flake of dried food off her mother's almost hairless black head. Mrs. Mostabi weighed eighty-five pounds, with wrists like small sticks and little bust under her gown. Blind, quieted by disease, and bedridden, her soul was already slipping free of her body.

"I'll be here with you for many hours per day," Laurie explained, speaking in that way the dying sometimes inspired—melodious, slow, economical—like talking to children. "I am here to help any way I can."

Tess asked questions, Laurie answered, Mrs. Mostabi like a table between them upon which they laid out their strategy.

Toward the end of the conversation, Laurie moved to begin her check of bedding, urine, and fecal bags. She pulled Mrs. Mostabi's covers back, preparing to check under her gown for the catheter immersions.

Seeming a little nervous, Tess said, "Have you ever spent time in Africa?"

"No," Laurie responded honestly, pleating the covers neatly back.

"Or spent time with African women?"

"Not really," Laurie responded, now lifting the elderly woman's gown. She paused a second, realizing she didn't know why Tess had asked.

"We're all built the same." Laurie smiled reassuringly. *Was Tess feeling modest about her mother? Would she want to leave the room?*

"Yes and no," Tess responded, helping with the gown. "You'll see."

Speechless, Laurie saw genitals, shaved perhaps a month before, a slight stubble growth of gray, very normal. But beneath them was a flat scar where the clitoris should have been, this scar visible because most of the labia had been sliced off as well. Mrs. Mostabi, far away on the morphine, lay unselfconsciously as her nurse saw scarred stitching holes all over the lower half of the vulva. Mrs. Mostabi's private, most sacred folds of flesh were vestiges of mutilation worse, in some way, than the cancer in her bones.

"Male nurses," Tess said, with horrible nonchalance, "seem to react less badly than female."

Laurie did not respond, trying to hide her horror.

"You've read about this but never seen it," Tess said frankly.

"Yes . . . uh yes, I guess so." Laurie quickly checked both catheters and replaced the gown over the old woman's groin.

5

Laurie felt angry as she looked up at Tess again, angry at Tess, at Mrs. Mostabi, at Muslim men. *Control yourself,* she soothed, moving her gaze back to the blind woman's eyes.

Laurie looked at Tess and raised her eyebrows, hoping she sounded calm, professional. "When was that done to her?"

"She told me she was eleven at the time of the ceremony."

"Ceremony?" Laurie could not hold back anger. "Jesus *Christ.* Those men should be shot. It's worse than rape."

Tess looked down at her mother's hands. "The men in her village knew little about it. It was an affair of women."

"No. It was . . ." Laurie gestured toward the ceiling, as if a bearded God were there. "It was men. Your mother could have died. Jesus."

"She did not think she could live unless she joined in this ritual."

Suddenly, shocking herself out of anger, Laurie wondered if Tess had . . . experienced a similar mutilation. She couldn't ask. But her face must have spoken.

"You wonder if I've been involved in this too?"

"No."

"I haven't. I was born in America to a father who, though I never knew him, would certainly not have wanted it. Most fortunate for me was the fact that my stepfather, who understood these things, made sure my mother did not succeed at it."

"Your *mother* wanted you to . . ." Laurie couldn't finish. She had heard of mothers betraying daughters—but like this?

"Mama had the other women set up, and they had me naked from the waist down, held down, and the doctor was washing his hands. My stepfather came rushing home from work—someone had told him. He screamed and beat the doctor and locked my mother in the basement."

"My God."

"I tell you this because I have been thinking about it since I called the hospice." Tess turned away, her eyes watering.

Laurie's anger was not replaced as she saw Tess' grief and embarrassment, but it shifted. She approached Tess and touched her arm. Tess reacted at first only by staring at her mother. Then her shoulders shook, and she began to sob. The rain poured outside the small window, imbuing Laurie with a sense of bleakness, like sound in an empty drum. She held the older woman, breathing deeply, recognizing, as she closed her eyes, that she was here now, fully here, in this particular house of the dying, each house unique in its unopened rooms of mood, pain, and memory.

* * *

Laurie began the drive to her apartment on Capitol Hill in a lessened rain and arrived an hour later, under a half-moon ringed by clouds. She pulled up to her curb and stepped out of the Honda Civic, locking the door behind her and taking off her coat. Without the rain, she now felt the humid warmth of the late spring evening. As she opened the front door of her apartment building, she was grateful that on this case, she could leave for home at ten p.m. every evening. Tess, though untrained in the health-care field, insisted on fulfilling caregiver duties from ten p.m. to ten a.m.

At home that night, inside her one-bedroom, second-floor apartment, she grabbed a Diet Coke and sat at her computer. The clock read 10:47. Like a journeyer travelling increasingly away from her safe home, Laurie moved from website to website, remaining online for nearly four hours. As she learned more about genital mutilation, she was filled with anger, and with sympathy. One website estimated twenty million victims, half of them in Africa. Another estimated double that number.

What is Islam? Laurie wondered with outrage. *How could a religion harbor, even encourage, these atrocities?* The websites said that female genital mutilation was not Muslim at all, at least not in doctrine. But Laurie did not see Jews, Christians, or Buddhists practicing it.

Another website talked about male circumcision as somehow equivalent to female circumcision. Hardly, Laurie thought angrily. Men wanted a piece of the victim pie, but they could wait in line.

At 2:23 a.m., standing on her back balcony, Laurie looked up at the Big Dipper and shivered at the image of Mrs. Mostabi's ravaged genitals. She felt educated now, but not reassured. She went back inside, put on her long flannel pajama shirt, and brushed her teeth, still consumed by rage, and worst of all, rage at women. All the websites agreed that it was *women* who kept this practice alive.

Laurie wrote in her journal, always her last ritual before sleep: *"I've given up on men. You already know that. But today hurts my faith in women."* She was tired and nearly turned off the light, but then she wrote: *"How is real human love possible? Show me that, and I'll know I'm home."* She closed the book, turned off the light, and lay back, her mind replaying, as it often did, former romantic relationships that had not worked, the cruelty of men, and now new images from the world of black-faced women, adding to the palimpsest of aloneness in the drifting dark.

* * *

"How was your night?" Laurie asked Mrs. Mostabi, who muttered in what Laurie assumed to be a dialect of Somali.

Tess answered for her mother. "Pretty serene. We got some sleep."

Laurie checked vitals, thinking, *I will have to bathe her today.*

"Do you mind if I ask what she's saying?" Laurie said to Tess.

Tess listened. "Something about a dance and a chair. Her cousin Kafile—something about him, in a room." She smoothed out her mother's sheet. "She's a very wise woman, my mother. I wish you had known her . . . before the cancer."

Dressed in blue jeans, a white pullover, and black pumps, Tess looked like she'd spent time this morning to put on a good face, but her eyes seemed heavy. She'd had a hard night.

"I wish I had known her," Laurie said automatically, moving to check the IV.

"She had many gifts."

The drip was set. Laurie finished changing the urine and fecal bags below the bed rack and moved to the catheters. She pulled the sheet down and gown up. This time, as the lost labia and scarring showed, she tried to do her work without emotion, though her hands trembled. Laurie pulled out the catheters and replaced them with new disposable ones. Her fingers could not help but further crush Mrs. Mostabi's disused but grotesquely memorable vulva.

"I once thought about being a nurse," Tess said. Laurie knew Tess had retired a year ago from a long career of office management in law firms.

"Tessie?" The sound was a coarse, accented groan. Laurie and Tess turned immediately to Mrs. Mostabi, who was now awake, eyelids half open.

"Yes, Mama?"

"Who is there?"

"The nurse, Laurie Fuller. She's fixing you up."

Mrs. Mostabi talked slowly in her language. Tess, moving her own head down to the older face, like a flower on a stem sagging forward, answered her mother in Somali. She gently clasped her mother's emaciated bicep with her right hand.

"She says that you have a tender touch," Tess reported to Laurie.

"I hope she'll think so when I bathe her." Laurie forced a laugh, replacing the gown and sheets over the old woman. Now that Mrs. Mostabi was awake—fully present—Laurie felt the nighttime's confusion and anger again.

"She wants you to have some jewelry," Tess reported, after another back-and-forth in Somali. "I'll get it for you." Tess moved toward the door. "Don't worry. It's very normal. She gives people jewelry all the time. It's customary."

"No, I can't accept!" Laurie insisted. But Tess was gone. "I shouldn't, really, Mrs. Mostabi." Laurie turned to the old woman. "Your family already pays us."

"You are how old?" Mrs. Mostabi asked.

"Twenty-five, Mrs. Mostabi." Laurie had to bend down to hear the hoarse voice.

"Young, you."

"Yes."

"You have children?"

"No," Laurie replied.

"No children? Very sad."

"Well, not exact—"

"You have husband?" Mrs. Mostabi interrupted.

Laurie laughed. "Oh no. And I might never have one."

Mrs. Mostabi sucked in breath and seemed to shiver. "Don't say that. Bad luck. You must have husband."

"I don't think I must."

"Why?"

Laurie tried to take a friendly tone. "I guess I just have an

. . . intuition about it. Actually, I don't think I'll marry or start a family."

"You can see future?"

Laurie instinctively shook her head, forgetting for a second that the gesture was lost to the old woman's blindness. "Let's just say that I don't think any man will ever really know how to love me. I've tried with men. Maybe I have what people call 'high standards.' Or maybe I don't really like men as much as a woman is supposed to."

Mrs. Mostabi seemed to try to smile through her sickness and pain. Her lower lip shunted slightly to the left. "So young. You don't know truth."

Talk was so good for terminal patients, and Laurie knew to try to continue it with Mrs. Mostabi, though she felt a lecture coming on. "What truth, Mrs. Mostabi?"

The old woman went quiet, then breathed in as deeply as she could. Her voice came out like a loud whisper.

"You not born to *be* loved. You born to love the other ones."

The old woman was going into that old-fashioned stuff that drove Laurie nuts.

"A woman is born to love her man, serve her man, not get her own needs met."

Better to be silent, Laurie thought.

Mrs. Mostabi did not hear anything negative in the silence. She chose her words deliberately. "We come . . . here . . . we live . . . we come to give love. Only to give love. Only this . . . important. Not take. To take love not important."

Tess came in holding a gold bracelet, etched with tiny triangles. "Here you go, Laurie."

"I can't take that!" Laurie cried, feeling its weight. It was real gold.

"You take that," Mrs. Mostabi murmured firmly, breathless from too much talk. Laurie gave the bracelet to Tess, turning to her patient, automatically moving her hands to the wrist.

"You take!" Mrs. Mostabi exhaled, opening her eyes wide, agitated. Laurie had to say yes or rile the patient. She could work things out with Tess later.

"I'll take it," Laurie reassured. "Thank you, Mrs. Mostabi. It's so beautiful."

"Thank you," Mrs. Mostabi said. "Thank you." Her pulse was fine, but she had three days left, maybe two. Death was near.

*   *   *

She needed to return this gift, but how? Laurie called her supervisor to find out what was ethically acceptable. The patient absolutely wanted the gift accepted—and Tess insisted too—but company policy clearly stated that a hospice nurse couldn't accept gifts that were probably going to end up as part of probate. This gift, quite valuable, fit that profile.

"There is obviously a cultural element here," her supervisor concluded. "Worst of all would be to offend, at this sensitive time. Try to give the gift back, but it's your judgment call if the patient and the family won't take no for an answer."

They wouldn't, and so the next day Laurie wore the bracelet to the house—shining obtrusively on her white skin, she thought. Tomorrow, she resolved, she'd wear a long-sleeve blouse with her jeans. She had spent hours that night searching websites on Islam and on Africa for information on gift giving of this kind. She'd discovered that many Muslim thinkers claimed their religion was "the great world religion of peace." *Peace? Muslims seemed to love war*, she thought, *except on these websites*. Yet there were so many beautiful passages in the Quran, and the religion did not seem completely savage, especially in its five sacred acts which did indeed include generous giving. She was stuck with keeping the gift, no doubt.

"I'm so glad you'll be wearing it today when 'the maidens' come," Tess said with a smile. "Mama will be so thrilled!"

The maidens, Laurie learned, were a group of Muslim women, Mrs. Mostabi's best friends, all in their seventies—Isabel Gorku, Alina Amelikinian, and Cossi Sally Toputu. 'None have husbands to speak of' was the strange way Tess had put it. This was Tess' way of saying that one husband was dead, another had divorced, and one had returned to Iran, probably remarrying there but not dissolving his marriage here. Alina had not realized for a full two years after her husband had left that, in this country, *she* could dissolve the marriage. It had taken her five years after that, Tess related, to decide that Islam would forgive her for finding her own way to freedom.

"The maidens come every Wednesday at one o'clock," Tess warned, her voice betraying both a bemusement about them and a yearning for their presence. "The hospital couldn't stop them, and I know they'll be here today."

Mrs. Mostabi was sleeping, her somnolent vocalizations increasing, the sweats coming more frequently, her eyes rarely opening. The morphine drip, set up for both self-service and external control, was depleted appropriately.

"Pain awakens us," Tess had said upon Laurie's arrival that morning. As Laurie checked the morphine bag to make sure it worked, and pointed out how little had been used, Tess recreated a Somalian proverb of some kind. "*Pain awakens us. Happiness puts us to sleep.* I guess I'd rather sleep!"

Laurie had argued with that philosophy. "I think I'd rather be awake, even if it means pain." But Laurie knew she argued like a young person would, luxuriating in the abstract when, in fact, there was no doubt in how Mrs. Mostabi found happiness now—not by wakefulness, but by drifting away from life.

When the attending physician left just after ten a.m., he confirmed what Laurie saw clearly—Mrs. Mostabi had begun to move into constant unconsciousness. That perhaps her last major lucid moment involved the giving of a gift to a stranger made Laurie even more sure, in the end, that she had to accept the bracelet.

Sleeping is how the maidens found their dying friend, and this did not please them.

Isabel Forku, seventy-nine, a tiny blackened woman with curly gray hair in a net, thick glasses, and a cane, seemed nearly to shout at Mrs. Mostabi. "We're here! You shall not yet go, Lila! We're here!"

Ms. Amelikinian, the Iranian, her silver hair cut short, her neck draped with gold, her wrinkled brown face caught in a frozen smile, apologized for her friend's loudness and spoke more soothingly to the dying one.

The largest of the women ("Call me Cossi Sally, nurse, not the 'Mrs.' word, and not Sally") at least two hundred pounds, five-foot-ten, imposing, even to Laurie's tall height, and the ringleader, took Mrs. Mostabi's hand and squeezed as if to break it. "Has Imam come by here?" she asked Tess.

"Last night. Late."

Imam, Laurie had learned from the internet, was like a preacher.

"Will he come again?"

"Not before she passes," Tess said, quickly wiping a tear from her right eye.

"It is our job now," Cossi Sally pronounced, satisfaction in her eyes.

Was there some resentment about the Imam not returning? Laurie wondered. She thought she saw anger in the eyes of all these Muslim women—at least she hoped she did. To her, the Muslim men in these women's lives, whether Imam or their husbands, seemed like the Muslim men Laurie knew from college, always seeming to come and go as they pleased, confining, restraining, even savaging women. Laurie stood just to the side of these dark-skinned women and hoped she could at least be one of them in anger at the men. She hoped also that none of these women had ever wanted to do to their daughters what Mrs. Mostabi had wanted to do to Tess. But as Laurie watched—protectively wanting to tell them to back off, let the patient be, stop squeezing her so aggressively—she had the terrible feeling that all these women were completely baffling and somehow savage.

"What does the nurse say?" Mrs. Forku asked Laurie.

Laurie, caught off guard, frowned. "About?"

"She means," Tess interpreted, "how long does mother have to live, in your opinion?"

"I can't say, really—"

"What does doctor say?" Mrs. Forku interrupted, turning back to Tess.

"This is America," Tess responded. "No one will speak their mind about death."

"I think it is soon," Mrs. Forku announced. "Twenty-four hour. We will not leave here much."

The other two women nodded. Cossi Sally seemed to chortle. She had made this sound five or six times already, in response to words around her. It reminded Laurie of her image of an African-American gospel churchgoer. In the movies there was always this responsive verbalizing, this grunted acceptance or disdain.

"Will you all be staying here?" Laurie asked, realizing that Tess may have made up the guest rooms earlier in the day, not for the family arriving the next day but for these women. In many of Laurie's cases, people moved into a house for the last days or hours. Laurie wondered what a house full of these women would be like—not solemn, certainly.

"I hope so," Tess said, looking in turn at each woman, receiving an affirmative nod or grunt. "I'm glad! Mama would want that."

Laurie felt like the foreigner here. She always felt like an outsider in a hospice home—that came with the work—but in this house she felt especially askew.

"Let's give Mrs. Mostabi some rest and quiet," she suggested firmly, breaking into the circle of black bodies surrounding the bed and taking the emaciated wrist to check her patient's pulse.

"Oh, she'll have quiet soon enough!" Cossi Sally laughed, not moving.

"Come into the kitchen," Tess said. "I've made some sandwiches."

As the maidens filed out, Mrs. Forku called out encouragingly to Mrs. Mostabi in her native language.

Forcing levity into her voice, Laurie said to Mrs. Mostabi, "You have nice friends." She smoothed her patient's sheet and touched her forehead. It was clammy, cool.

Laurie knew she didn't have to protect her patient from friends and family, but she felt a pressing urge in this case to do so. She knew she needed to control that urge—it was not appropriate for a hospice nurse, even one who had stumbled into a world of women so irregular and disturbing. She could get in real trouble here, the kind of trouble one never saw coming and never fully understood.

II

"Do you remember how you met her, Isabel?" Cossi Sally asked between bites of a curry dish Alina had made. The sky outside was darkening. It was nine-thirty, almost time for Laurie to go home.

The maidens had bustled about and talked and laughed and sung songs around her patient all day. Laurie had called her supervisor again for advice. "It seems cultural," was again the reply. "I think you must give physical care to your patient and otherwise stay out of the way." Even the jingle of jewelry was loud in this house—all the women covered with gold and silver, Cossi Sally's long ears sagging with heavy earrings, like the statue in the living room.

In response to Cossi Sally's question, Isabel said, "She gave me a book. We met like that."

Mrs. Mostabi had met all these women and immediately given them things—Cossi Sally a cooking pan, Alina a ring.

"This she gave you?" Cossi Sally asked, pointing to Laurie's bracelet.

"Yes," Laurie said as she fingered it.

Tess, sitting next to her at the table, touched her arm. "I think Laurie is a bit overwhelmed by us."

"No, no," Laurie protested, though perhaps Tess suspected all the calls to her supervisor.

"We'll make a loud noise to welcome death," Cossi Sally informed her.

Mrs. Forku nodded. "A loud noise."

Alina was quiet, eating the chicken-raisin curry.

"Lila is the wisest among us," Cossi Sally said as she smiled at Tess and reached a big hand to touch her cheek.

Tess leaned her head toward the touch. "I'm so glad you are here, all of you," she said. Then Mrs. Mostabi made a loud sound in the other room, and all heads turned. Laurie jumped up first, got around the corner into the room, and to her patient's bedside.

Mrs. Mostabi was awake. Her eyes glimmered as she heard the company.

"How are you feeling?" Laurie asked, expecting no answer except the watering eyes, the lolling head. The other women came in now.

"Lila?" Cossi Sally asked, touching her old friend's head. "Can we get you anything?"

Laurie picked up the plastic glass and straw on the hospital table beside the bed. Mrs. Mostabi let the straw touch her lips but drank little. Laurie touched her lips with ice from a tiny ice chest. All maidens' eyes were touched by tears as the rain fell outside. Laurie gently offered the water again, but Mrs. Mostabi refused.

Tess reached for the water cup, and Laurie relinquished it, stepping to the head of the bed to prop up Lila's head for a drink. Tess had no better luck with the water and put it back down on the table.

Cossi Sally said, "You are the wise one, Lila."

"Yes, you are," Mrs. Forku nodded.

"*Allahu Akbar*," Alina whispered to begin an Arabic prayer.

Laurie recognized it from her research, everyone but herself now murmuring along with Alina. Laurie was filled with a strange calm as she listened to this alien but graceful song of words and women's voices.

"God is great," Cossi Sally confirmed when Alina was done.

As Laurie lifted her eyes, she saw Tess glance at her. Laurie wondered if she should stay the night. She thought it possible Mrs. Mostabi would pass very soon.

"What came here?" Mrs. Mostabi cried out suddenly, her voice hoarse.

"I'm here, Mama," Tess replied. "And the maidens."

"What came here?" Mrs. Mostabi repeated, eyes closed. "What came here?" They were delirious vocalizations.

"It is us, Lila," Cossi Sally repeated.

Mrs. Mostabi was eating and drinking so little that her brain had shut down. Laurie lifted the lid of the ice chest on the bedside table and, with tongs, passed a piece to Tess for her mother's lips. Tess caressed the brown and red-lined lips until her mother turned away.

Mrs. Forku began speaking in Somali, but Mrs. Mostabi did not respond. She had dropped off to sleep and her breathing was stertorous.

All the women stood a moment in silence. Then Tess, noticing the ice melting in her fingers, blinked tears from her eyes and placed the ice in the bowl.

"Maybe I should spend the night," Laurie offered Tess, who responded with a preoccupied nod.

Mrs. Forku and Cossi Sally walked out and back toward dinner, Alina following, then Laurie, who sensed that Tess wanted a moment alone with her mother.

"Do you like our cooking?" Cossi Sally asked as they sat back down.

"Absolutely," Laurie responded, digging back into the curry.

"But not our traditions, maybe?"

"What . . . do you mean?" She felt her stomach knot. *Was it so obvious?*

"You fidget while we pray. You uncomfortable?"

"Did I fidget in there? I'm sorry." She ate another bite.

"Tess say you hate the cutting."

Laurie raised her eyes to Cossi Sally. *Jesus! Why had Tess told them? It was such a betrayal.* "The cutting?" she temporized.

Cossi Sally did not respond. She took a bite of her food, the silence grating.

Laurie found herself hardening in it. *Why be afraid here?* The worst she could do was offend. Maybe women who bought into all the Muslim crap needed a little offending.

"You know" she said, putting her fork down, "I was hurt by seeing it. I'm sorry, but that was my experience. I felt hurt."

"It is a sacred thing," Mrs. Forku corrected her. "You can't understand it."

"I wish Tess hadn't said anything to you." Laurie cocked her head back toward the hallway and toward Mrs. Mostabi's room.

"You think you know what love is, young woman?" Cossi Sally asked.

Laurie flushed a little, resenting her reaction. "Of course, I do." Her voice came with sarcasm, uncontained, unprofessional.

Mrs. Forku grunted. She was always grunting. *How irritating*, Laurie thought.

"We clean Lila from now on," Cossi Sally said. "Not you. We touch her. Not you."

Laurie's mouth opened, but wordlessly. All the women looked at her with disapproval. *I'm her nurse, for God's sake!* she wanted to yell. Who were they to say she was unempathetic, incapable? When had Tess told them her discomfort? It must have been just before dinner. They had sure hidden any discomfort well, chatting away throughout the meal.

"Laurie?" Tess called from the doorway. "Can you help me a moment?"

Laurie pushed her chair back, dropped her napkin on it, and called an acknowledgment. When she got to Mrs. Mostabi's room, Tess was standing with her sleeping mother.

"I heard. I'm sorry that I spoke to them. We talk about everything, the maidens and I."

Laurie could not voice her feelings because she did not understand the rules and boundaries among these women.

"You're in good hands," Laurie said. "And it's my time to go anyway. You have my beeper. If she gets much weaker, call me."

"I will," Tess promised, putting out her hand, as she had done so often, as if a handshake would be forgiveness.

Laurie shook the outstretched hand, then avoided the maidens as she gathered her things and went out the front door.

* * *

Laurie fell to sleep like slipping into water and entered a world not her own. There was a village of mud and adobe buildings and a well beside a dirty, grassy path. There were women and girls walking but no men. All the women were as black as Cossi Sally. Laurie followed a group of women, as if pulled along by a sense of things to come. They filed along the path toward a hut—brown, wet-walled, roofed by reams of hay and grass. Inside the hut was a girl on a wooden table. She wore a white nightshirt above her waist, naked below, her black legs spread open. There was a strap across her belly. Two large, black women wearing long, floppy gowns and red turbanlike headdresses held her legs. The girl, about twelve or thirteen, was crying with more grief than fear. Despite the tears, Laurie could hear that the girl was humming. Some of the women were humming too. In her right hand, a huge woman with a yellow headdress carried a circumcision tool with a knife-sharp circular end; in her left, a spool of black thread. Laurie

21

heard the terrible rain and the humming. She saw the tools of pain and she saw the shaved groin of the girl. She tried to reach out but could not move. The large woman was murmuring as she moved into position, the girl's groin encircled by women. The girl's legs jerked, and the woman at her head pressed a rag into her mouth. She screamed, but it was drowned out by the sound of rain.

Laurie broke the surface of sleep, her body shooting up in bed, her heart thumping in her chest. For a while, she was still in the hut, in that moment when the nightmare is over, but the dreamer has not let go.

"Jesus!" she cried aloud. Her top sheet and comforter had been tossed aside during sleep, as was the professional journal she'd been reading. Her long Tommy Hilfiger t-shirt just covered her torso and panties, her legs pale and naked on the lavender flannel sheets. Images from the dream coalesced with images of her bed and body, and she contemplated both until they separated again and she was fully awake. The red numbers of her digital clock read 12:31.

Laurie breathed deeply the relief of someone saved from evil. She pushed her legs over the side of the bed and then moved on the cool wood floor to her bathroom. Why had she felt inadequate with Cossi Sally and the others tonight? They were in the wrong, she in the right. Laurie sat peeing and felt a rush of resentment at her supervisor's mantra, "It's a cultural thing." *Damn him! "Culture" was no excuse.*

Laurie pulled her panties up, trudging back through the darkness to her bed. Cultural or not, she would confront Cossi Sally tomorrow. She would fully express her feelings—politely, professionally, but firmly.

"Sally," she would say—to hell with the double name—"You can live like primitive people if you want, but don't make me feel bad for thinking genital mutilation is wrong!"

Laurie stood in the dark room, rehearsing. The rain fell unceasingly against her bedroom window, distorting her mirror-image like a Seurat painting. She ranted at the big black woman, then mellowed her performance. She mustn't appear crazy. As she found the right tone, the sound of the rain wrapped her words in professionalism that was compassionate yet firm.

When she felt prepared enough, she climbed back into bed, her anger becoming fatigue and then sadness. For after all that rehearsing, after finding the perfect tone and words, she knew she could not attack the old women, or even correct them. It was against professional ethics. These old women were living their lives during their friend's journey into death, and Laurie had to hold her tongue.

Closing her eyes, Laurie thought about Muslim men, realizing just how much these men scared her. Black men were frightening, even if exotic, and black Muslim men were more frightening than anything. Though she was athletic, confident in her body and her strength, she avoided these men, especially when they walked in groups. She did not think herself different from any woman in this regard, and that irked her.

Laurie breathed deeply, trying to relax. She hated the fear of men. It was an anger and a grief in her that raised its head after every broken relationship. Tonight, it appeared without even a broken heart to beckon it. Laurie hated being afraid of anything. She hated, too, when her head would not shut out images, memories.

Laurie could not stop the images—of the African girl writhing in pain; of her own mother and father standing together in a photo on a Hawaiian beach before they died; of her aunt and uncle who tried so hard to raise their sullen niece; of Tess being rescued by her stepfather from her mother. Mrs. Mostabi's words—something about being here to love others, not to be loved—echoed in her ears. Laurie yearned for her bed to rise up and embrace her like a living being. She wanted to cry.

It was almost dawn, but Laurie could not sleep. Finally, she resorted to masturbation, which sickened her a little, given the subject of her dream, but at least it allowed her some release. At four-thirty, lulled by the sounds of the rain, the whirring of the refrigerator, and the hum of the furnace, she finally drifted off, wishing she did not have to return to Mrs. Mostabi's house.

But only seconds later, it seemed, the alarm rang.

III

Laurie untied the thin string at the back of Mrs. Mostabi's white gown, revealing her naked back. She kept her left arm under her patient's waist and rolled her face up. With her right hand, she gently pulled the gown from around the resettling shoulders, leaving Mrs. Mostabi's wrinkled body completely naked. Tossing the gown onto the chair beside the bed, Laurie grasped the cloth in the warm water and wrung it out. Mrs. Mostabi murmured and stirred. Laurie reached for a piece of ice for her lips and then tried to offer her water. Mrs. Mostabi turned away, turning away from life. Laurie knew this would be her last bath.

The maidens had been quiet toward Laurie this morning and let her give her patient this bath. Touching her gently, Laurie washed her thin legs, long breasts, and the rough skin of her belly. Then Laurie moved to the groin, parting the legs slightly and closing her eyes against the carnage. She caught herself in this sudden, self-imposed blindness, and opened her eyes again. She washed the long-ago bruised and still scarred labia, urethra, and vaginal walls.

"Still, you cannot look."

Startled, as if caught in wrongdoing, Laurie jumped.

Tess had taken Alina and Mrs. Forku shopping for groceries. Cossi Sally had been left snoring in the other room, but suddenly here she was.

"I'm . . ." she turned a second, then steadied herself. *"Screw you!"* was what she wanted to say, but instead she remained focused on her patient. "I'm bathing my patient, obviously."

"This I see."

Laurie finished the groin, replaced the washcloth in the bowl, then brought both arms back to the body to turn her over. Cossi Sally came to help, moving Mrs. Mostabi as easily with her bulk as Laurie did with her athletic build.

Laurie murmured thanks, then began on the shoulders. Mrs. Mostabi sighed, a sound somewhere between breath and silence.

"She is beautiful always," Cossi Sally stated. "Everywhere on her is beautiful. Everywhere."

Laurie stopped washing. Was Cossi Sally taunting?

"You think I'm wrong for having feelings about mutilation," she said to the huge woman. "I understand that. But I *do* have feelings, and they won't go away."

Cossi Sally smiled, touching Laurie's nose with a pudgy finger. "I think you have many feelings."

"I do. Look at this poor woman."

"I look at myself. See the same thing."

Laurie was silent. What could she say?

"I'm not sorry, girl. I know how to love. You see that? Mrs. Mostabi too. We're not sorry."

"You get cut up so you can love someone?" Laurie countered. "That's the logic?"

Cossi Sally frowned, either not understanding or just not rising to the bait.

Laurie reached for the clean gown on the chair beside her.

"I will help the lonely young nurse dress my friend Lila," Cossi Sally said with a wry grin. She did now seem to understand what Laurie had said and was putting Laurie in her place.

Laurie chose a high-road response. "If you wish."

Together, like two women dressing a sleeping child, they crooked each arm, caressing each hand through and into the short sleeves. They lay the gown over the body, pushed it under each side like tucking in a sheet, then gently turned Mrs. Mostabi over. They straightened the gown, then Laurie tied the shoulder line, Cossi Sally the hip line. Again, they turned Mrs. Mostabi face up, and Laurie inserted the catheters. Mrs. Mostabi sighed, and the sound made both women pause at the bedside. Neither woman said anything, yet their fingers nearly touched as both reached, instinctively, toward Mrs. Mostabi's neck. Then Mrs. Mostabi breathed again, and Cossi Sally let out a sound that was half giggle and half sob. Her face betrayed a hundred emotions. A vulnerability, a glance at death, transpired behind her eyes, and Laurie felt a bond, like a passing grief between women.

"Can I tell you what Mrs. Mostabi told me?" Laurie asked, feeling no compulsion to leave the bedside, feeling as if this were the place to stand right now. "Will you explain yourself and explain her to me, a dumb American, even if you don't like me?"

Cossi Sally smiled, tossing her head so her necklaces chattered. "You say wrong. I do like you. Now what did the wise woman say to you?"

"The same thing you said."

Cossi Sally seemed not to understand, so Laurie recreated her only full conversation with Mrs. Mostabi. "She seemed afraid for me, that I would not marry. I said no man could keep up with me, love me. And she said, he didn't have to love me. That didn't matter. It only mattered if I loved him. It was that old traditional stuff."

Cossi Sally patted Mrs. Mostabi's thin arm with her huge hand. "Yes. She say that."

"But why?" Laurie challenged. "Can't she be loved too? Shouldn't we all find someone to love us? Most people say that's why we're here—to find someone. I don't know if I believe that altogether, but at least I do know that I can't let myself be cut up, just so I wouldn't be tempted to seek love for myself. Right? Isn't that what you and Mrs. Mostabi are saying about this . . . tradition? That your place is to give love, not get it?" Laurie had leaned forward over Mrs. Mostabi and she apologized, pulling back slightly. "I'm sorry I'm so intense."

"So many questions," Cossi Sally frowned as she shook the bracelets on her wrists. Laurie realized she may have spoken her words too quickly. But while she thought how to simplify, Cossi Sally leaned down to Mrs. Mostabi's forehead, touched it gently with her palm, then kissed it. When she straightened back up, she said to Laurie, "You kiss too."

"Me?" Laurie thought perhaps this was an honor of some kind. "Why?"

"Too many questions. You kiss the wise woman."

Some magic thing, maybe? Kiss her and see the light?

"I don't think it would be right," Laurie said. "I mean, I'm her nurse."

"You too proud to kiss the wise woman?"

Proud? How little Cossi Sally understood. Didn't she know about professionalism? But then again, there was the huge face, those black eyes, so challenging. What could it hurt to kiss a forehead?

Laurie leaned over and touched her lips to the damp, fragile skin.

"I think you a very proud woman," Cossi Sally nodded. "It make you so desperate. No humble in you. No humility. No awe."

"Like, be humble and let myself be mutilated?" *Damn, the words came out fast!* Laurie heard the chip in her own voice with immediate regret.

Cossi Sally just sighed, as if at a young girl. "One day you understand. Remember you kissed the wise woman. She will teach you, even after she die. Her spirit always in your pocket now."

"In my pocket," Laurie repeated politely. "I see."

"I go watch television," Cossi Sally announced. She turned away and walked out the door, swishing and jangling.

As Laurie returned to her chores, she recalled a boy with whom she'd been desperately in love when she was seventeen. He was a born-again Christian, and she'd become one too, he accepting her mainly as a "best friend" rather than a lover. What a strange few months of her life! His community became her own immediate family. Two months into the mainly platonic relationship, she remembered she kissed his hand at the prom—a costume ball that year, he dressed as a prince, she a princess. How vulnerable she felt, in that simple gesture. And how far she'd moved away from it, and from any dependencies like it in college. In the end, the boy had graduated and left for the military, and she left his church, finding in college a new independence, new vision, new strength.

"Come quick, Laurie!" Cossi Sally suddenly called from the other room. "Come see this!"

Laurie left the bowl in the sink and walked quickly through the corridor to the den. Cossi Sally sat on the couch, pointing to an image on the television from a soap opera. A handsome, blond man and pretty, buxom blond woman were kissing passionately.

"You see?" Cossi Sally pointed. "You see?"

"They're kissing. I see that."

Cossi Sally seemed genuinely frustrated, trying to communicate something. "There is no love there. You see? They kiss, but no love."

It looks pretty loving, Laurie corrected silently. But then she saw what Cossi Sally was saying. She saw mainly lust, not love. The kiss, the hands in each other's hair, along the back and shoulders, the murmurs of passion—they lacked real love. They were just play acting. *Is that what the woman meant?*

"You see, yes?" Cossi Sally spoke triumphantly.

"I guess so." Laurie nodded. She was ready to say something more, but then just let herself watch. The couple now moved away from the kiss—the woman to the phone, the man to some papers. Now it was even clearer how little they actually loved each other.

"I don't think it right no more, what my mama did to me," Cossi Sally closed her eyes, reaching to hold Laurie's hand with a sweaty palm. "I live in America now. I know a woman a free soul now. No more this cutting for you girls. This cutting not really Islam. I know that. I not stupid. But I glad this much. I know why I live. I never lonely. I always know love is my breathing. I can give it all the time. All the time! Because I never wait for it. You see? I never wait. I surrender so I never wait."

Cossi Sally opened her eyes and said, "You too lonely, girl. Too lonely! Yes? You know, yes?"

Laurie smiled, her palm wet and squeezed too tight. "Maybe I should become a Muslim!" She gently pulled her palm back. *I'm alone, maybe*, she wanted to say, *but don't categorize me as lonely*.

"You?" Cossi Sally laughed. "Muslim? You, independent girl!"

Laurie laughed. "That's true." Wouldn't Ruth and Chloe and the others from college die to hear her say "Muslim" in a positive way.

"But maybe Islam in you," Cossi Sally continued. "Maybe you resist. Islam very good for you. So much love."

Laurie smiled politely and then smacked her hands on her thighs. "Better get back to work." Despite the instinctive move, she didn't really want to get up. She wanted more . . . of what?

Cossi Sally laughed, turning back to the TV. "The wise woman in your pocket now! Oh yes, Laurie."

Strangely, Laurie felt something just then, a warmth, or something near her. She stood a moment, as if looking for it. Her stomach was knotted and her throat constricting. Something danced in her mind—something so powerful—what was it? She couldn't find it. But she felt it, just felt it. It felt like truth.

Cossi Sally was still grinning, watching the commercial, as Laurie moved away and out of the room.

Laurie went back to the bathroom, back to clean-up, her throat choked. Maybe I'll miss this house a little, she thought, clearing her throat, swallowing. She swiped her right hand across her eyes, clearing phantom tears. She realized she felt somewhat afraid as she wrung out the washcloth at the sink, then dropped it into the laundry hamper. Afraid? Nothing had happened. Yet her stomach was in butterflies.

Mrs. Mostabi in her pocket? What strange feelings. There was the murmur of the television in the other room, and her whole body in some kind of pain, but no clear certainty of what she felt.

Laurie finished her clean-up work and went back to sit with her patient, watching the morphine drip, listening to Mrs. Mostabi's soft breathing, and holding back tears as she held the old woman's small hand.

IV

It rained in torrents the day Mrs. Mostabi died. She lived two days longer than Laurie thought she would, and she was put to rest the day after her passing. Driving to the cemetery, every car window steamed, windshield wipers flapped unceasingly. At the gravesite, maple trees dripped tiny bullets of rain onto raincoats and umbrellas.

After Laurie spent that time alone with Cossi Sally and Mrs. Mostabi, Tess, Mrs. Forku, and Alina returned and cooked a large meal, making extra food to accommodate the family members coming in from out of town the next day. Laurie had gone home that night to a restless sleep, yet she did not feel very tired as she drove back to the Marshall house following Tess' call to say that her mother had passed. Laurie always felt moved when a patient died, and today more so than usual. Tess told her that her two grown children were already there, with many grandchildren.

Even though Tess asked her not to ring the bell but always to just come in, Laurie knocked as she entered. A huge black boy saw her first. He was perhaps thirteen, but already at least five-foot-ten and 200 pounds.

"I'm the nurse." She smiled. "Laurie."

"Jonathan," he said, his accent pure teenage American.

In the living room and hallways, there were several adults and at least a dozen children, every age represented. Some wore colorful clothing from Africa, some wore regular American clothes. As Laurie introduced herself to a woman about her age, she suddenly heard a wail from the bedroom, and then Tess calming someone down.

"Grandmama died just a few hours ago," the woman said. She wore an orange cap and orange muumuu-like dress but spoke with no accent.

"My condolences," Laurie said immediately. "She was a wonderful woman."

Laurie excused herself and moved toward Mrs. Mostabi's room where a black woman was weeping loudly. Two men stood near her with beads in their hands. They kneaded them, one of the men murmuring to the weeping woman, the other to himself. Tess stood with Cossi Sally, rocking in each other's arms.

Laurie felt immensely Caucasian, like a whale caught on shore. "Tess," she whispered.

Tess turned, searched her eyes for a moment and, seeing the tenderness of acceptance, wrapped her arms around Laurie and wept. Comforting the blind woman's daughter, Laurie felt all eyes suddenly upon her and lowered her head.

At the funeral, all eyes were on the speakers—the Imam, then Cossi Sally, then Tess. The African women in attendance murmured even as the speaker at graveside spoke. Laurie had learned that Muslims usually did not allow embalming, instead wrapping the dead in special cloth shrouds and burying them quickly, before decay set in. Mrs. Mostabi's closed casket sat over its grave in a Muslim section of Seattle's Memorial Cemetery, thirty-six hours after "the wise one"—a phrase often repeated by speakers today—died.

Laurie had felt quite sad since the death. She felt she could not speak for the constriction in her throat, but suddenly here at the gravesite, she could not cry either. Perhaps, she thought, she was all cried out. There was nothing left.

"My mother gave everything to her life," Tess was saying. Cossi Sally and another woman each steadied Tess' arms with the press of their hands. A lot of the speeches, including the

Imam's, had been in African languages with Arabic prayers. Tess had begun in her mother's native language but now spoke English, presumably for some of the great-grandchildren who might not be learning the native tongues. "She was willing to sacrifice everything for those she loved. I will miss her so much."

Tess began to sob, and she was held by Cossi Sally, another woman, then two children, and then the physical shuffle of others around her. Her family and friends crowded around, keeping death and sadness in so tight, but somehow holding at bay whatever could be worse.

* * *

"Thank you for all your help this week," Tess said to Laurie back at the house, her hand shaking as her daughter handed her a cup of tea. Evening had come, lights were on in the house, rain was still falling outside.

"You bet." Laurie smiled, thinking how many times she had helped the dying and the bereaved, but never a group like this. The house teemed not only with sadness, but with delight. Two teenage boys played chess on an ornamented table, their legs nervously bouncing as they bit their nails. A number of men stood around them watching. Smaller children ran around the backyard, despite the rain and dark, playing soccer in the illuminated field of a backyard floodlight. The girls and women occupied themselves mainly with each other, and with cleaning up.

"You won't forget us," Cossi Sally declared with kindness.

"No," Laurie admitted, "I sure won't."

The hospice nurse, especially when needed only for parts of four days, did not remain a friend of the family. And in this strangest of cases, Laurie knew when Tess called with news of the death that her relationships with these women would now also die, and she felt a terrible hardness in the pit of her stomach.

"You call Cossi Sally any time you like?" the big woman offered. "Any time. I am here, or somewhere about."

"I will. You've taught me many things," Laurie said amiably. "Yours is a different world."

Cossi Sally, so serious, responded, "Maybe we've taught you. Maybe not. Lila is in your pocket. You will see."

Tess said something in Somali to two little girls, who giggled and went to the kitchen. A teenage girl came up to Laurie, speaking in a perfect American accent, but wearing a traditional Muslim *abaya*, her head wrapped in a gray scarf so no hair showed, the rest of her body covered, her shoes sturdy and black.

"Do you like being a nurse?" she asked.

"I do. Yes."

"It's hard for me. I want to be a nurse. But . . . it's hard."

Laurie had learned there was prejudice in Islam against nurses because they touched dirty bodily fluids and because they touched naked men. This was disdained.

"Maybe you could become a doctor," Laurie offered.

The girl nodded, but not in agreement, and walked away.

Laurie felt alone. She wanted to stay but knew she must leave. This was no longer her place. And in less than a week, hadn't she had more than enough stretching of the self? She sensed she'd been changed by these people but didn't know how. It was frustrating but hanging around wouldn't help. It was time to move on.

She said her goodbyes—to Tess, Cossi Sally, the other maidens, myriad others. And she said goodbye, in the direction of Mrs. Mostabi's room, to the sweet old woman. As Laurie walked through the people and the sculptures, the paintings and the mystery of another continent, she remembered Cossi Sally and the television soap opera, the affection and wisdom in the huge woman's eyes. Cossi Sally did not look after her, turning to Tess in grief. Laurie felt herself become a stranger here once again.

She left the front door open behind her, her last words spoken, ironically, to the huge teen boy who had greeted her less than two days ago in the rain. "Goodbye," Laurie said simply. He nodded, then closed the door behind her.

In the car, she waited a moment to see if Tess, Cossi Sally, Mrs. Forku, or even the teen girl would appear. After a minute or two, she started her car, revved it, and pulled away, her windshield wipers tossing the rain only to be inundated seconds later. As she turned the corner, she felt tears coming to her eyes. Laurie resisted them, but they overwhelmed her. She sat at the red light as tears filled her eyes, her body rigid. When the light turned, she pushed the gas pedal and glided forward, a tear dropping onto her right cheek. She had to pull over.

Images of Mrs. Mostabi's ravaged genitals played, suddenly, in her mind. It was for this pain she thought she wept this quiet rage of tears. Then images of her mother and father filled her mind, filled it quickly like water rushing into a hole. She saw her mother looking down at her, tucking her in. She saw her father, his craggy face lit up by a reading lamp. She saw the two of them talking at the dinner table. Were these memories? Were they real? Were they the fantasies she had concocted during her adolescence, composing a childhood with parents out of fragments of sight and sound?

A car pulled up alongside hers, the woman on the passenger side peering in at her. Laurie, sobbing, turned her head away, waving with a raised hand, praying they would move on. She had not sobbed like this since the last time she went to her parents' graves, five years before. Their gravesites came into her mind now, and her tears mixed with a feeling of shame, of betrayal, and of loneliness.

Laurie saw the big boy at the doorway. She saw all the children, the parents, the grandparents, the aunts, the uncles, the cousins. There was so much family there. Not one person in that mix understood, she suspected, what aloneness really felt like.

And now, as her sobs turned to a kind of melting of her face and body; as her arms shuddered, her palms clamped on the steering wheel; as her head fell forward and sounds came out of her throat like the sounds of an animal, Laurie knew why she sobbed, and could do nothing about it. She saw herself as Tess or Cossi Sally. She saw herself as her aunt. Such kind women, each in their way. And each alone for so many years after husbands died, and yet none of them knew how it was to be alone because all could boast children in their memory, and in their lives.

Just a few months before, when Laurie had visited her aunt, now a widow living in Florida, the kind woman had said, "The greatest thing I ever did was being a mother to you." Recalling this, Laurie cried out, "Oh God," her heart in her chest pumping so fast she thought she would go into arrest. Laurie could not remember a time she had felt this completely lost, unable to control herself . . . except for the moment, when she was about seven, that she finally understood her parents would never return.

"Oh God," she cried out. "Help me." There was only the echo of her voice in the rain-drenched car.

Laurie wiped her eyes on her coat sleeve. Her nose and mouth were a sluice. Another car seemed to be slowing toward her. She had to do something, get control. Laurie sucked inward, her nose and throat burning with phlegm. She could not remember if she had any Kleenex in her purse. Inching the Honda forward, her blurred eyes on the road, she rifled open her purse zipper, then groped inside. She felt tissue, pulled some out, touched herself, her eyes first, to clear her vision. The road lay before her, her lane clear. She accelerated into it, the murmur in her mind, *I just have to make it home.* She forced herself to drive, pulling up to the streetlight at the West Seattle bridge. She breathed in deeply again, her tears beginning to lessen.

Breathing carefully, four or five times, she felt equilibrium returning. As the light went green, and she pushed her accelerator, she brought Mrs. Mostabi's face into her mind, then Tess, then Cossi Sally.

"Okay," she murmured, "I don't want the bizarre kind of love all the blind Muslim women have. But I envy them. Shit!"

She accelerated over the bridge, pulling onto I-5 North, traffic thicker now, but moving, a river of red taillights. Images of Tess, Cossi Sally, Mrs. Mostabi fled into the rain and red taillights. Laurie tried to grab the images back, as if instinctively grabbing a friend falling off a cliff. They disappeared. Then Laurie thought, *Just as well.* For she was driving, alone, through the rain, that African world not her world, its people alien to her. Why, she wondered, with all the homes of the dying she had befriended, should she envy this one? Why had this one broken through?

Laurie kept driving through the rain and the metronome of the windshield wipers. She found her exit off the freeway, moving through the patterns of streetlights, curbs, sidewalks. She turned on her radio, to a commercial, turned it off again. Arriving at Broadway Avenue, she found her alley, pulled her car into its spot. The rain still fell in torrents, but now she was only a few feet from the entrance to her apartment building. She locked her car and ran the short distance in seconds. Climbing the stairs, entering her apartment, she turned on the hallway light, pulled off her soaked pumps and pantyhose, and stood for a second, tears dried, alone in her hallway, as if mesmerized by nothing but air and light.

Laurie found herself moving toward the phone in the darkened living room. It was as if she was carried not by herself but some other force. She touched the gold bracelet on her wrist, preparing to take it off, but then letting it embrace her bones. She still knew her ex-boyfriend Mark's number by heart. Dialing it, she waited for a first ring, then a second, then hung up. She dialed her aunt, whose machine answered.

"It's Laurie," she intoned, hearing the crack of emotion in her own voice. "Don't worry. I'm fine. Just call me, would you? Call me late if you have to. It's okay, I'll be up."

She placed the phone back in its cradle, kneading the gold bracelet. What would it be like, she wondered, to live your life not to *be* loved, but to love others? It would be like total detachment from desire, from yearning, from desperation. Cleansed by tears, embraced by the sight and sound of rain, touching the gold bracelet like an amulet, Laurie found herself seriously confronted by the murmurings of the blind woman, Mrs. Mostabi. How could any of this make sense? Yet it did make sense somehow. Didn't it? What all those women believed—if you took away the savagery—was some kind of profound truth. How could Laurie feel so close to it, so close to understanding the heart of it, and yet so completely far away?

I'm the one who's blind, she suspected ironically. If only her aunt would call. She could always talk to her aunt, though her aunt rarely seemed to hear her niece, her disappointment always expressed silently.

Laurie dialed her aunt's number again, then stopped. She hung up the phone, lifted it, dialed Tess Marshall's number. She would talk to Cossi Sally. What would she say? What would she ask? Hadn't Cossi Sally tried once already to explain, using a television soap opera? Laurie hung up the phone again. She set the phone aside and sat silently.

Laurie pushed off the couch and onto her carpeted floor. She turned back to the couch and leaned there, elbows crooked, palms together pointed upward in prayer, the way her parents and her aunt and uncle had insisted she pray at bedside.

Silently, eyes closed, Laurie said the Lord's Prayer. Then, aloud, she murmured, "It's been years since I prayed, but I'm praying now. I can't really tell you why, but I guess I just have to. I need help. I need help. Every time I help someone die, I get better and better at not being sad, but it's all just a defense. I'm full of shit."

This was a strange humility, Laurie thought. This whole thing, kneeling here. She already wanted it to end, but she continued it, mustering every prayer she knew from way back. She felt comfort in the series of moments, even as her knees hurt and her body yearned to step out of the wet dress. She felt a serenity in it. She felt thankful for the bowing of herself. All this surprised her.

"Dear God," she said, "I'm hard as a rock. I'm dense. I'm young. I need help."

In kneeling, in praying, she felt lightness, as if she could fly. It was a feeling of beauty and grace that seemed to spread throughout her, like a tingling after great laughter, or a sudden insight after great pain. She felt she could float if she wished. It was as if she were not quite here, kneeling at the couch with the beat of rain outside. She seemed to be somewhere else, so filled with happiness.

Laurie felt laughter rising in her, a quick sudden burst, uncontrollable. She let it come, her face melting in smiles. It was as if she were being held in a dance of absolute love and compassion. A fleeting voice in her mind, more than once, tried to invade the feeling of joy and peace, but the feeling was so complete, so rapturous, that even her own mind was powerless.

"My God!" she murmured, touching the bracelet. It must have magic! She felt so good.

She stood, giving relief immediately to her knees. She reached back to unzip her dress, stepped out of it, then her bra and panties, and moved toward the bathroom and the shower. She was freezing cold now, and the water warmed the chill that had, in the last few moments, invaded. She realized she had been on the floor for at least five minutes, watery with life like the rain and lit like the lamplight, completely one with every inch of cloth, every sound, every memory.

Laurie let the water run down her breasts, her flat stomach, her pubic hair, and down through the surface of her genitals. A shiver went through her. She stood in the water long enough to warm up, yearning already to pray again, there at the couch. She knew she prayed to a crazy God who struck the beloved down and ravaged women, yet Laurie knew she must pray again. As the water heated Laurie's body, she washed herself and then stepped out, back into the cool air, dried and found herself, in her towel, on her knees again at the couch, holding the gold bracelet Mrs. Mostabi had given her, yearning for it to hold power, to hold magic again.

It did. The feeling of beauty, the lightness, the grinning on her face was still there. It was all such an immense rush of electricity. What could it be? It felt like her parents were with her, kissing her on the cheeks and arms and face. She found herself singing "Amazing Grace," then trying to sing or hum the songs the Muslim women had sung.

When the phone rang, Laurie was saying, "Thank you, Mrs. Mostabi, for coming into my life," and lifted the receiver. She held the gold bracelet in her hand, her hair up in a towel, her body wrapped, the rain receding outside.

"Laurie, are you alright?" It was her aunt's voice.

"Judith!"

"Laurie, I got your call."

It was strange to try to talk. "I had this strange case, an old woman . . . sorry I haven't called in a while. Judith, I'm sorry."

"I'm just glad you did. Are you alright?"

Laurie paused, trying to think how to explain. *What good were words? What, really, had happened?*

"I think I've just . . ." Laurie couldn't go on. *Just felt God?*

"Laurie, what's the matter?"

Laurie was a rush of words, lying in her towel on the couch as she spoke, describing the funeral, all the black people, the beautiful dying woman, the ravaged genitals. Her aunt listened, and even days later Laurie would remember how telling her aunt about Tess, Mrs. Mostabi, Cossi Sally, and all the rest had felt like part of the praying she was supposed to do.

And that was what she told Cossi Sally, three days later, when she arrived at the Marshall house, under a bright blue sun, still touched by wonder and hopeful as the young can always be, who meet their demons enough to know that where there is a demon, there might be the shape of angels. She told Cossi Sally and Tess that something had happened to her the night Mrs. Mostabi was buried, some new feeling in her she thought was hope, and the women embraced her lovingly, and Laurie embraced them.

When her aunt next saw Laurie—she flew up to Seattle a week later—she was prepared for her niece to be dressed completely differently, in Muslim clothing. Judith knew from phone calls that Laurie had been experimenting with Islam. She prayed the *Salat*. She responded to the call to prayer, *la ilaha illa allah, there is no God but God*, with the *Fatiha*, hands folded respectfully at her heart before she prostrated herself. When she bowed, prostrate during prayer, she said she bowed into the ocean of God. But when Judith greeted her niece at the airport,

Laurie was dressed as always. Her aunt, who had always loved her, wept, not tears of grief but tears of joy, for Laurie seemed what she had never seemed before—happy.

Laurie assured her aunt with a hug that she was not becoming a Muslim, but she said she was enjoying "a new sense of God," in her words. Even before finishing her hug of greeting, Laurie showed her aunt Mrs. Mostabi's bracelet, gold and shining.

"So, this is it," Judith exclaimed, admiring the slightly ridged designs.

"I think Mrs. Mostabi is always going to be with me," Laurie said. "I know it sounds weird, but I really think so."

Laurie said she could not wait to have her aunt meet Tess and the maidens, but for Judith's part, when the meeting did come, it seemed to her the black women were a little confused by Laurie's intense interest in them. They were gracious, however, providing the white women with a busy tea of African cakes, a hard paste like falafel, and lots of chatter in Tess' backyard, under a cloudless, sunny sky.

When Laurie returned her aunt to the airport, promising to be in better touch this time, Laurie was aware of feeling that not only was her beloved aunt leaving, but also that she could not return very often to Tess and Cossi Sally, and that the brief leave of absence from work she had asked for and taken, must now, after a month, come to an end. It was time to drive up to another house, time to enter the process of dying again. But this time, she thought she would do better at it all. Could there ever be a greater surprise in any house she entered than Mrs. Mostabi's destroyed femininity and the wisdom that came from it, wisdom Laurie sensed she still did not fully fathom, yet wisdom that now she felt like a caress on the cheek.

Laurie returned home from the airport and phoned her supervisor. He was glad to have her back and said so. "Thought we were losing you there," he said on the phone, trying to wonder after her well-being without really asking.

She thanked him for his understanding and accepted her next assignment by moving to her computer and downloading, a few minutes later, a new file on a new patient, Jo Lynn Belsky, seventy-eight.

She printed the file but, before she read it, Laurie moved quietly to the couch, where she dropped to her knees, gentling herself in prayer and noticing, not unhappily, that it had begun to rain outside, water dripping in tiny rivulets on the window where many nights ago she had stared out into the darkness after a terrifying dream.

Fingering her gold bracelet, Laurie spoke to her mother and father. "The Muslims have done it. How, I don't know. But I'll be alright now."

And for the first time in her life, Laurie Fuller believed she would be.

necati bey

When I left Turkey, Necati Bey didn't notice me go. He had stopped being present in his shop at the times he knew I would come. His son, who was taking over the business, invariably stood in his place—politely, firmly—and sent me on my way.

"Can I at least speak to him?" I would ask. "Is there a problem?"

"No, no. No problem. My father is tired today." Or, "My father sends his regards." Or, "My father is back in his workshop, not to be disturbed."

Necati Bey sold copper and brass bowls, figurines, trays, belts, lanterns, canteens—some of them very old, but most of them new. He did the pounding and chiseling decoration on these objects in a workshop down an alley nearby. Often, I walked alone there, hearing the clanging of countless similar workshops. Sometimes I thought I heard his particular chiseling in the cacophony and moved a little faster toward his door. But when I arrived at the window of his place, looked through the glass filmed with a transparent patina of dust, noted the fire in the red coals, tools heating at the fire, a half-drunk tea on the edge of the worktable, yet the place otherwise empty, I saw—or imagined I saw—a whiff of steam rising from the tea glass, as if he'd suddenly left everything, escaped.

Once, just after sunset, I went into the empty workshop. I cleaned off a gritty stool and sat, waiting. Men walked by, stepped in, chatted, left again. The son appeared, asked me why I was there.

"You said he might be here," I reminded him.

"But won't you please leave?" he asked. "You know everything. There is nothing left to say."

With my hands folded over a package on my lap, I remained where I was, rudely silent. The silence gave me, I hoped, an air of being insulted, of holding back righteous anger. The son, in his middle twenties, just a few years younger than I, wanted neither to insult nor to confront me. My problem with his father was, after all, not his business, and he might have sided with me in a way. A father can be an enemy when you are young.

He murmured that he would try to find his father. I said I would wait until he did. Twice he came back, looked in, saw me still there. Thirty minutes passed before he gave in. He brought his father to the door, and Necati Bey walked in from the noisy, darkened street.

"You've been avoiding me," I said, putting my package in front of him on his worktable. "Why?"

He said nothing.

I motioned to the package. "I've brought you something."

"Very kind," he said without looking at me. He put on a glove, picked up some tongs which were red-hot in the coals, and tossed them against the cooler, ashen side of the open kiln. He pulled a chisel off a nail on the wall and put it into the coals.

"You're not going to open it?" I challenged. "It's a valuable gift."

I had bought him something he'd often admired in a shop in another part of the city during our walks together, a Syrian backgammon set inlaid with mother-of-pearl. It was not too expensive for me, as my consulting work paid very well, in dollars. He could tell by the shape of the package what the gift was. But he showed no interest. He pushed the chisel tool farther into his embering fire, and I felt tired suddenly. I looked at the side of his head and thought, "Alright, let go of it, let this man be." Then, as if free of something for now, I turned and took the two steps to the low, rickety door and went out into the alley. At least, I rationalized, the backgammon board would always remind him of my attempts at friendship.

I wasn't more than thirty feet down the alley when I stopped short. I turned quickly, not believing what I'd suddenly thought. I came to the edge of his window. There he was, not furtively, not angrily, more like a workman patiently at his task, feeding the gift into the fire.

*   *   *

Necati Bey was a tall, quiet man, with a face that sank in the middle. His forehead jutted out, all the way down to his eyebrows, but then, until the bony, protruding chin, his nose and mouth and cheeks sank inward, curving his lips into the expression of a smile. Because the nose was flat and the eyes close together under the ridge of the brow, his face looked like that of a skinny clown, difficult to take too seriously. Since he was nearly seventy, wrinkles added to the picture, crinkling deeply whenever he gave a true smile or laughed. I'd never seen anyone quite like him, never seen, especially, a forehead overhanging the face like a deep awning.

Even he joked about his appearance, saying that at his birth his father—who was delivering him in a wheat field with the help of an older brother—must have put his hand in the canal and connected too forcefully with the soft new skull. Drunk on raki one night, Necati Bey also claimed that when neighbors came to both congratulate and console the family—for his mother died shortly after his birth—he, only a few days in the world, could see and hear everything perfectly, as if he were already an old man.

"What did you see?" I asked, also drunk, playing along. "What did you hear?"

"I saw myself everywhere," he waved his hand. "My face was in every face that stared down at me. Very painful, this was, very strange. Then I went to sleep for many years and woke up one day as a man. What do you think?" He downed the milky, white raki left in his glass, nodding his head at what seemed to him a real memory.

Perhaps I should have said something profound or sensible, but I was drunk, and I said, "You are one crazy weird guy!" And we laughed together. I said this to him many times over the months, and he seemed to grimace in his pleasure at hearing it.

I met Necati Bey like any of his other customers. I went into his shop, communicated using the few words of Turkish I knew, and pointed at items that interested me—an Ottoman copper bowl, a village canteen, brass candlesticks. He tended to me politely and wrapped them, asking if I spoke German. His English, he said, was poor. I apologized for my poor Turkish and answered happily that I did speak German. As it turned out, we'd both lived in Hamburg for some time. As it also turned out, both our great-grandfathers had emigrated to our respective home countries—the US. and Turkey—from Russian Georgia. We seemed to find many connections between us. We found that we held some similar opinions on contemporary Turkey. These connections were not enough, certainly, to explain our quick and strong friendship, but they were its starting point. We spent many afternoons and evenings together over that winter, visiting tea houses, restaurants, bars, and playing backgammon in his shop. "I've always been old," he said once, "but you make me feel young. You know how to laugh."

"You give me something to laugh at," I said. "You're great." In fact, he was so energetic, a tall, old, gangling man skidding me around his city. It was he who made me feel young.

There were, of course, times when the mood seemed to shift, or his family shot me questioning glances, and Necati Bey himself seemed to recede inward, all of us eating silently at the family table, as if some silent struggle were going on which I couldn't comprehend. I asked his wife once about it, but she said everything was fine. I asked his son in the shop, on the sly, while Necati Bey was down the street at the toilet. His son shrugged, saying, "It will pass."

I asked Necati Bey about it one day over the backgammon board as we sat next to the wood-burning stove.

He laughed. "Why do you think of problems? Families will quarrel. It's nothing." And he stood up, motioning for us to trade seats, warm our other sides.

I said, rising, "But maybe you're spending too much time with me? Maybe your family is jealous of me or something? I don't want to make trouble."

He laughed. "It's in your English, isn't it? Where you say, 'Talk about the devil and he'll come.'"

"Of course," I nodded. "And in German, it's similar, as you know."

"Yes. And in my Turkish, do you know what we say?"

I shook my head.

"It will interest you. Maybe it pertains to you even," he said, his eyelids flickering for a second as he worked on the translation. "We say, *'Kopegi an, sopayi hazirla.'* Maybe we could put it like this. 'If you mention the dog, you should prepare the stick.' This is like the devil. If you speak of it, you must confront it. Why rush to confront something? Maybe it isn't even there in the first place."

There was nothing wrong with his wanting privacy, I decided. We would not mention the dog again. Let his family problem be his own.

"We'll talk of something else," he said. "Have I told you about my journey to Mecca in the fifties?"

Again, I shook my head.

"This you will find very funny. You've noticed, of course, that the door to my house is painted green? This means a male member of the house went to Mecca. That member was me. Now I, and my father, we grew up in a time when religion was losing its power to secular things in Turkey. Of course, it still is controlled in our country. But every once in a while, an Imam is a great orator in a community, attendance at his mosque increases, and he makes pleas for men to fulfill the great vow of Islam, the pilgrimage to Mecca. My father discovered this Imam first—I don't remember the man's name. He took me and my friend Ozer to hear him. One thing led to another, with my father encouraging like a bird on the shoulder, and finally Ozer and I decided we would make the haj. We would see many places on the way. We would see Syria, Damascus, Iraq, Baghdad, Arabia, and we would fulfill this vow, because who knew, maybe it would be useful after all to fulfill a sacred vow? You don't know what awaits you. So, we went.

"I will never forget all the people we met. They mix in the head, but I remember them. We went to so many villages and towns. I first saw the mother-of-pearl backgammon sets in Damascus. I wanted one very much, but I certainly was not a rich pilgrim. And not only did I have very little money, but would it be appropriate to buy a fancy set while on such a pilgrimage? Of course not. One is supposed to go himself to Mecca, not with a hundred things dragging him down. So, we went our way."

He observed me. "It seems funny to you. You turn up your cheek."

"No, no," I said. "Not that you didn't buy the set, that seems right to me. I just got an image in my mind of someone dragging all sorts of *things* behind him on a dusty road. That would definitely defeat the purpose of a pilgrimage."

"That's how I felt. Ozer thought we should buy the set, but we didn't. Anyway, it's not this that's funny. It's how I felt, how *we* felt, Ozer and I, when we finally finished with buses and hitchhiking and strange cities and places, and when we came to the walled gates of Mecca. Why do I think you will find this funny? Because you must see the two of us there, standing in awe, heart-struck, like young lovers, walking among the others around us, walking in the grubby, long- traveled crowd through the gate and into the holy place. We were in awe! You are a young man, not at all religious—this awe must strike you queerly, two young men going without much sense in their heads to this place, and now they are suddenly awed by it."

I laughed. "It isn't so funny. It often happens. I've felt awe in Jerusalem, I suppose."

"Then perhaps you understand. We stood there with our mouths open so the flies could get in, looking at the walls and gardens and mosques. I was young, when laughter comes so easily, and I remember Ozer and me, we laughed after we came back out of the holy place. But there was a certain feeling I had there, inside, a very ancient and terrible feeling. I never had it again. It was my whole self for a moment. Why am I telling you about it?" He laughed suddenly, wrinkles shifting and eyes alert. "I should be telling my son, shouldn't I? Why tell you? Come on, let's play some more backgammon and call for more tea."

He stood up quickly and went out, called for the tea boy, and came back in. There was a misshapen, brooding expression on his face. "Perhaps we should laugh at the silliness of the human spirit," he said.

I agreed. "A little callousness is healthy."

"Perhaps," he nodded, pondering me. We finished the game in silence. I felt a terror in my gut; no reason for fear to be there, but in the silence, it was. We started a new game and the tea boy came. Necati Bey tipped the boy well, thanked him, opened conversation again as if nothing had happened. I must come to his house, he said, for dinner. Yes, come this evening. Yes, it would be a surprise to the family, but they wouldn't mind.

*   *   *

Later, I would blame the bowl I gave him that evening for our troubles. If I hadn't forced it on him, I decided, everything would have been different. We parted at five, and I promised to come to his house by nine. I went home and took down an old Ottoman fruit bowl I had just bought on a trip to Istanbul. I had bought it with Necati Bey in mind, knowing that he would be able to tell me the approximate year it had been made and the quality of the workmanship. The bowl was an antique, at least a hundred years old, and would have been very difficult for me as a foreigner to take out of the country. Because of foreign theft of Turkish antiquities over the years, Turkish laws on the matter had become strict. I was going to give it to him in a few months anyway, just before I left for the States, but I decided to give it to him that evening. Without knowing why, I felt I owed him something, and it should be something valuable. Perhaps I had a premonition.

The bowl was quite heavy, thick copper, tinned inside for use with food. Etched and chiseled into the outer surface were simple, elegant lines and latticework. The bowl itself rose up and out from a small platform, indented in the middle all around, then rose out again. I smiled in the taxi at the thought that I had, quite unconsciously, chosen a bowl whose forehead and chin jutted out and whose middle face sunk inward.

I arrived at his house at nine and was greeted, not warmly but not indifferently. I pulled the bowl out of the plastic bag, set it on the table. "I've brought something for the family," I said.

Fusun, the wife, picked it up admiringly, thanking me, and carried it to Necati Bey, who sat in his usual chair. He scrutinized it under the lamp beside him, turned it up and down, and traced the line work with a finger. He nodded admiringly and thanked me. Fusun and Esim, the daughter, told me I shouldn't have brought it. Necati Bey smiled and said that I must be thinking of something—the bowl's workmanship was so good, it put his own to shame. I disagreed, of course, and Fusun told him not to be silly. His son came over to the lamp, picked up the bowl, and asked where I'd gotten it.

The evening passed amiably, although Necati Bey kept going back to the gift, pondering it. Did I, through the bowl, bring the evil eye into their house, as Fusun later claimed? Now, as I look at all of them in that dining room, see them on the screen of my imagination, I see the copper-red, line-decorated, one-hundred-year-old fruit bowl at the center of the table, harboring there some sort of black magic, emitting murkiness into the clarity of their lives. I can actually see the darkness; it is palpable.

I saw it when, a few days later, I went to Necati Bey's shop and found him with customers. He and the middle-aged Turkish couple spoke in rapid Turkish, the couple acknowledging me with a polite nod, Necati Bey not reacting to me at all. He seemed to be telling them that what they were looking for was in another shop, took them past me out the door, disappeared with them into the street, and did not return for at least the half hour I waited. I left, angry.

I went back to the shop over the weekend, and Necati Bey was polite but too busy to play backgammon, he said. I left again. I went back a week later, and to my surprise, saw the Ottoman bowl I'd given him on the top shelf, slightly hidden, but definitely for sale. I didn't mention it to him, tried to interest him in talk or backgammon. His son came in and told him he was needed down the street. Necati Bey left, and the son told me he had to lock up now, would I mind leaving. Only three weeks later, after more futile tries, I was in Necati Bey's workshop, giving him the Syrian backgammon board.

I had thought, after watching the board burning in the kiln fire, that I was done with that obstinate old man. But now, four years later, I'm thinking about him. I'm seeing myself in a wheat field delivering my child and accidentally punching the center of its face flat in the birth canal. I'm seeing it look up at me from inside its diapers and tiny shirt, as if it were already old, a Necati Bey, hiding from me.

Now I remember a conversation with Murat, Necati Bey's son, one afternoon a few days before that last murky glance through the workshop window. I had gone into the shop to find Murat with his favorite newspaper, *Hurriyet*, spread out on the table in front of him. It was a Friday afternoon—I only worked at our company office a half day on Friday and always got to Copper Alley by four. Today, I had decided, I'll have it out with Necati Bey. What was I to have out? I didn't know. Why was I even angry, unhappy, confused? There seemed no reason, nothing I owed him, nothing he owed me—yet I knew today would be the day. But Necati Bey wasn't feeling very well, according to Murat, and had left the store in Murat's care.

"He's doing this more and more, lately," I said. "You must be pleased to have the responsibility."

"I am pleased," he confessed. "I've been waiting." But he cut himself off. "I can give you tea, if you'd like."

"Of course," I said. And he went out to call the boy. He limped on his right leg, a man shorter than his father, handsome, not as thin, but in the thick eyebrows and pointed chin there was a definite resemblance. His limp, Necati Bey once told me, was from a school-bus accident when he was a boy.

Murat returned, and I said, "Your father isn't feeling too bad, I hope."

"A little ill, that's all."

"Perhaps I will go to the house, then, and visit him."

"You would disturb him," he said.

"It's better I wait here then. Maybe he'll feel well this evening and return."

"I don't think so." Murat smiled wanly, clearly wishing I were gone. The door opened, and the boy brought tea.

"Would you like me to go and not come back?" I asked, touching the tea with my tongue. It was too hot to drink, both of us blowing on it, stirring our sugar in. "Tell me honestly."

"Honesty would be impolite, in this case," he said, taking a sip.

"Look," I said, setting the tea on the table away from me, "you tell me what's going on with your father, and I'll just get out of here. I'll never come back. It's that simple. Okay?"

He considered me, eye to eye. "You really do not know?"

"Of course not," I said impatiently. "I feel like a fool. Everyone knows, and I don't."

"If you don't know," he shook his head, "maybe you *can't* know. This is the kind of thing my father would say, isn't it?" He smiled. "Yes. You know the bowl you gave him? You remember it?"

"Of course, I remember it."

"Is it possible you searched and searched in Istanbul to find one that was better than he could make?"

"Is that what he thinks? Of course not. I searched for a gift worthy of him."

"This is as you see it. But the workmanship on the bowl is exquisite. It is better than his own work, he thinks. It is bad luck that you should be the one to give it to him." He took a deep drink of tea.

Something rang untrue, simplified. "And now he's angry at me because I accidentally gave him a very fine piece of copperwork? Which suddenly makes him feel his own work isn't worthwhile? I don't believe it. Your father has bitter feelings about something—maybe about you—and he wants to throw them off, so he's throwing them onto me. I'm not the cause of anything, I'm just convenient. What's gotten into him? I considered him a friend."

"He is an *old man*," Murat said with sudden emotion. It came out with a hissing passion that surprised me. "How could you be his *friend*? You leered at him, laughed at him. You always felt superior."

"What the hell are you talking about?"

"He told you things he never told anyone. He should not have done that. He told you about his birth face, and you laughed. You called him crazy—he told me. He told you about Mecca, and you laughed at him. He didn't like it. It hurt him."

"Christ, he wanted me to laugh. He was always aware of human silliness—he said this. He always laughed at things. What are you talking about?"

"You asked for an explanation, I have given it to you. He is an old man. He will not allow you to drag his soul out into the open. There will be consequences for everyone when an old man confesses his little shames. Now, are you a man of your word? Will you go and not bother him anymore?"

I stood up. "I don't believe this. You're telling me he 'opened his soul' to me? We had fun together, we played backgammon, we drank tea, we talked a little . . ."

"He talked, you listened."

"We *both* talked." But my hand dipped to my tea glass, my eyes with it, my stomach suddenly tight and hollow. He had talked, I had listened. Very rarely did I talk about myself. This was true.

I brought the glass to my mouth, gulped the tea down, set the glass back in front of Murat.

"Sometimes," I said, "things just go wrong. I'm a man of my word. I won't be back."

He thanked me. He came to the door, held it open for me, and put out his hand. We shook hands, and I turned away from him into the street.

* * *

I was not immediately true to my word, of course. I went back until, as I said, Necati Bey finally came that evening into his workshop. Often, over the last few years, seeing again on my inner screen that mother-of-pearl set in the fire, I've imagined myself as Necati Bey, making the trip by bus, car, wagon, tractor, unsure of why he was going to Mecca at all, crossing three countries. I've replayed the conversation we had that afternoon, replayed his telling of the story. I've found nothing hostile there, nothing terrible, nothing insensitive or insincere. I was not in any way morally culpable for the rift of our friendship. Yet, this morning, as I have the last four, I woke up sweating, having dreamt that my hand was in my wife's birth canal and our baby's face was ruined. What shall I do with that dream?

a desperate pride

Raf Horowitz arrived in Jerusalem carrying nothing of value. He had little self-confidence, little direction, and only an overnight bag. When his plane landed at Ben Gurion at eleven p.m., it fell out of mist, which he took as an omen.

His heart had been broken in San Francisco, had become numb on the 747, and now sought the darkness and inherent quiet of night. In darkness, sound traveled best, and Raf wanted to hear the sound of his own weeping, something he had not yet been able to accomplish. It seemed that the possibility of tears remained behind in San Francisco, as did any sense of home, of the past, or of Sheri.

Raf Horowitz landed in Jerusalem feeling not like a Jewish pilgrim but like a child abandoned. He hoped Israel could give him new life, for he had chosen to leave his old profession in biochemistry and, for a time, his own country. He had dreams now of writing poetry (as he had in college) of joining the Peace Corps, of doing something essential for the future of the world. But first, he needed to gain strength in this land, Israel, where his mother insisted that any Jew—even one recently dumped—could feel renewed.

"Raf, dear, would you get that down for me?" He turned to the sweet elderly woman who had tried to cheer him up during this London-Ben Gurion leg of the flight.

"Of course, Mrs. Abromowitz." Her suitcase was light at the handle end, but heavy at the bottom. "Hey," he chided, "what do you have, an iron in there?"

She grinned, toothy. Clearly, he'd been right.

Raf had made many trips abroad over the years, amazed so often to meet similar people on each.

"She says we can buy clothes anywhere," her husband chimed in, a man also in his seventies, bald-headed but with huge white eyebrows and a matching mustache. "But we can't buy an iron as good as her Sears iron."

Raf brought the suitcase to the floor and pulled the dragging-arm up for Mrs. Abromowitz's convenience. Sitting beside him throughout the trip, she'd wanted to know if he was all right. ("I can always tell when someone has a broken heart. Tell me what happened.") He told her about Sheri, about how long ago he had planned this vacation with her, about how he thought he would quit the biotech research he and Sheri had been doing for their dissertations, about how he had some money and was going to protect it for as long as he could here in Israel, about a new poem, a search for hope through language.

"You're a good soul," the old woman said as she took her suitcase handle in her right arm and touched his arm with her left. "I think you're cinnamon, dear."

Cinnamon? He smiled and thanked her. Raf had never been one to deny another human being her vision—but cinnamon?

"Good luck, Raf," said Dr. Lipner, a retired anesthesiologist, recent widower, and first-time pilgrim. Teary-eyed during the flight, he'd said, "I'm making the trip my wife always begged me to make. I think she's waiting for me at the Wailing Wall. It's going to be a new millennium soon. It was time I came."

At seventy-eight, he sensed magic in the air. A true pilgrim.

* * *

"Rafi! Get to the point!" Nafiza laughed, exasperated. Not only am I consorting with a Jew, she thought, but such a talker! No wonder this Sheri left him. If he wrote more and talked less, he'd actually make it as a poet.

"Sorry. Sorry. Tangential again." He always grinned when he apologized, his brown eyes glazing, his white teeth like a flash of light through the thick brown beard.

"Nafiza, I mean, look, I was just trying to create the scene. 'Pilgrim'—that's the key. Now, I'm starting to see my poem as being about a pilgrim. Dr. Lipner used the word, right?"

And he was off again, talking.

Rafi (she liked adding the soft sound of the 'i' at the end, making it more like her own original language) was like an escape, as Nafiza pondered him, listening. She drove her housemate Gadi's Ford Cortina toward Ramallah to see her family. Rafi was very kind and somewhat surreal. So American, like McDonald's, even though he seemed to think his Jewishness made him exotic in the States.

"In America, I'm a Jew in a Christian country. Here, in Israel, *I'm* the majority! I'm home!" Yes—like all American Jews, he took immediate possession of Israel.

"No, Raf, *I'm* home," she had corrected him, and he apologized profusely, as he was prone to do, his brown, puppy-dog eyes twinkling. Television, movies, Rafi—all an escape to give her graduate school life some fun and pleasure. And Rafi could give pleasure. A Palestinian girl with a Jewish man from America—this was fun. Muslim and Israeli men—worthless. American men—especially the artist types, visiting Hebrew University from Yaddo, or coming over from the States on grants—these Americans were sometimes the best of men—solicitous lovers, energetic, passionate. But this one talked so much!

"That's what I'll tell your folks," Rafi said, "that I'm a pilgrim. That I came here feeling lost, but once I understood that I was a pilgrim, I regained myself. We're all pilgrims. *That's* our common ground, whether we're Palestinian, Israeli, or American."

He was nervous about meeting her family, yet he insisted on it, almost obsessed for the last week. No matter how she tried to dissuade, he pushed.

"Nafiza, I never meet a girl's family soon enough. With Sheri, I was afraid to meet them, afraid they'd hate me. But not with you. I'm going to be fearless!"

You see yourself as a pilgrim, Nafiza thought. *I'll see you as an escape, because after today, things won't be the same between us.* She knew that, in the end, her family would blame *her* for letting his forceful, idealistic, Jewish naïveté into the house—especially now, with her cousins embroiled in Gaza with the Israeli fascists.

"And I still say, Nafi, that my poem will bring us all closer."

"No!" Nafiza chided. "You must not show it. I insist on that. Okay?" She wondered about her own vehemence. Could the poem really do harm? It was called *Making Peace with the Muslims*, after all, a kind of ode to hope.

"Sure, Nafiza." He touched her thigh, sending a shiver, squeezed, and grinned. "I got it." He reached a finger up her khaki shorts. He always had this on her. The sex. At that he was a far better poet than a man could ever be with words.

* * *

They had met just after he got in from the airport that first day, poetry at his pen tip. He had big ears, curly hair, and the flouncing walk of tall Americans.

"New guest this summer," her roommate Gadi had informed her a few days before. "From America. A distant cousin."

Gadi rarely said much, and Nafiza hadn't inquired. She was busy with graduate school—economics was a very demanding program, and she was the first female in her family to go to college, much less graduate school. Gadi's attic room was empty, and the house, after all, was Gadi's. How could she register anything but acceptance?

When she came in from the one-mile walk back from the university, around eleven p.m., she went to her bedroom and heard the clomping of a newcomer's shoes above her. Often with new roommates, she had to explain, "Please, no shoes upstairs. It's too noisy. I can't sleep." She went to the kitchen, got a snack, went back to her room, and changed into sweatpants and sandals, listening now to the heavy footsteps moving in and out of the little bathroom up there. Maybe the man—Raf from America—was just putting his things away. Maybe give him a *salaam*, a *shalom*, a "hi there", let him know a few house conveniences. Maybe slip in a comment about taking his shoes off when he walked up there.

She padded upstairs and did not have to knock, as the door was open. The man was quite tall and about her age, late twenties, pacing, laptop on the bed, a mesmerizing sight—six-feet four-inches at least, stooping at the edges of the attic ceiling. And dressed only in white jockey shorts! No fat on him. And no shoes, just a heavy walker. Like everyone in Jerusalem this week, he was hot, sweating worse because of the attic air. She couldn't blame him for wearing almost nothing. She, who rarely sweated, was wet with sweat. The oscillating fans throughout the house did nothing to abate the humidity.

Nafiza snuck away. *What a beauty!* Maybe an introduction later, though, when he had clothes on. Then one of the floorboards creaked under her foot. *Damn!*

"Gadi?" the man called in a deep voice, a lilting American

accent—not New York, like so many of the American Jews were, but something more compact.

Frozen, Nafiza stopped. Old instincts burdened her. He came immediately to his doorway at the top of the stairs, seeing her.

"Oh!" he exclaimed, startled but unselfconscious. He made no effort to cover himself.

Nafiza got her feet back and walked away without apology.

Dressed in a minute, in jeans and a blue T-shirt that read, "University of San Francisco," he came to her, apologizing. "I'm Raf. Sorry. I should have been dressed . . ."

She assured him that it was fine, and he followed her downstairs. And he talked! Some men were like that, Nafiza thought even then, talking a lot so they wouldn't be known, and so they would not have to know others. But this Raf talked about poetry, and Sheri, and microbes, and lost love, and soon they were walking onto the street. Once in a while, Nafiza spoke. She was used to speaking little, not only with men, but with women too.

"Can I read you a poem?" Raf asked. He wanted her in on everything, right away.

They were back at the house, his laptop on the kitchen table, Gadi eating a midnight snack (he never went to sleep before two a.m.), the box fans whirring. Raf, inspired in the last hour by an Ottoman miniature painting Gadi kept on the living room wall, had decided to scrap his "airplane poem" and start a new poem, about Ottomans, Muslims, Armenians. He read from it, hungry for response.

"But it's not about *you*," Gadi protested after about twenty lines. "You're not Armenian."

"Well, first of all, I do have a little Armenian blood, and I've been to Turkey and Kurdistan, seen the oppression. Jewish, Armenian, Palestinian . . ." Raf nodded toward Nafiza. ". . . all are victims. The Armenian here is symbolic of any and all victims of oppression."

Gadi shrugged, unimpressed.

In the country a few hours, and already Raf was arguing truth and art with an Israeli—a high-impact sport. Nafiza just listened, reminded of why she loved this land. No time for bullshit. Gadi got right to things. People's feelings be damned. Not until later did she realize Raf had felt hurt by Gadi. This American was more thin-skinned than a man should be.

And lying in bed later, she realized that she wanted the tall American. Sex, since she'd lost her virginity three years ago at twenty-two, had been a way of freedom for her—she never moralized about it. She did not get close to men in other ways, but she took what she wanted and gave a lot of body in return. She knew herself and knew men, and this Raf had a sweetness, a grief, and a hell of a body.

Three nights later, they made love. A week after that, Raf had read her all his poems, told her he loved her. Now, five weeks later, he insisted he meet her family. She resisted but then capitulated. This was her way, so often, when happiness seemed possible.

* * *

"Checkpoint," Nafiza interrupted him. "There."

Up ahead, cars were slowing, taillights awakening to red. The Israeli army had established checkpoints just outside the territory of the Palestinian Authority. Because the Cortina was driving to Ramallah, a center of unrest in the last six months, Nafiza had warned Rafi that security would be tight. "No problem," he'd said cheerily. "Next year is a new century. Things will be better."

Quickly, he had become accustomed to Israelis with shoulder-slung semiautomatic rifles and pistols strapped to their waists. Quickly, he had gone through the "I see it's true what I heard, even the women carry guns" phase, and quickly too—because he was this strange breed called American Jews, so innocent and pampered—he asked, "Doesn't it feel shitty to you, Nafiza, to see the Israelis act like kings?" And, "I wish you'd share more of your life with me. I know you've been hurt." And, "How do you do it, Nafiza? You're so forgiving, so assimilated into Israeli life."

But he did not seem to learn as quickly that she would not tell him about her childhood. She had not told anyone who was not an Arab woman. And even most Arabs did not learn from her the particular character of her predawn memories—a father taken, then returned by the Israelis, black and blue on both eyes and his lip swollen; a mother raped (by an Arab) when she was Nafiza's age; a brother beaten for trying to save his sister, little Nafiza, then fourteen, from rape by an Israeli. Arabs did not need to "share" nightmares with each other, nor especially did Palestinians. Each had enough of their own to last them.

The Israeli soldier, helmet on, his brow beaded with sweat, his black beard close-cut, came to the driver's window. He was a big man, box-faced, his left eye slightly more closed than his right. Nafiza carried a fanny pack rather than a purse. From it, she had already extracted her papers. Rafi had his passport out.

"Where are you going?" the soldier asked in Hebrew, a little flirtation in his twinkling brown eyes.

"Ramallah," she responded, as he read her name silently—*Nafiza Thara abu-Hussein*. She could see his shoulders stiffen, eyelids subtly close, lips tighten. Often this happened. She looked Jewish—as any Semite could—and enhanced the look by dressing Western. Thinking her Jewish, Israeli men often flirted with her, then learning who she was, felt a visceral betrayal, as if she had been an affectionate actor in his internal play. Some Israeli soldiers, especially now that young Palestinian men had begun a second intifada, had a special dislike of the Palestinian women who tried to cross over, for the Israeli men knew that unless she were a professional whore, she would not for a second let herself be open to his control.

"Your nationality?" the soldier asked Rafi in Hebrew.

"He wants to know where you're from," Nafiza translated.

"American, sir." Raf smiled, holding out his blue passport. "We're going to visit Nafiza's family."

The soldier raised his left hand, alerting Nafiza that he did not want her translation. He called for an English speaker from among two soldiers who stood smoking near a line of cars, open-trunked, undergoing inspection. One of the two broke away, coming over.

The squint-eyed soldier in Nafiza's face reprimanded her, saying, "You're stupid to take an American in with you. You should turn back."

"What's he saying?" Rafi asked. Now the other soldier was nearly there. "What's the matter, Nafiza?"

"Everything's fine. Don't get out of the car," she said firmly. Rafi would be the chivalrous type to turn this into an incident. He clearly noticed the soldier's hostility, and now he might want to get out and confront with words what could not be understood in words. Late into the night, in an Israeli police station, he'd be let go, a tourist misled, while she'd remain in a cell for some trumped up charge.

The two Israelis murmured between them, and now the new one, a clean-shaven, brown-skinned African flicked his cigarette away and bent close to her face. She could smell his smoke, sweat, and power.

To Rafi, in garbled English, he said, "Is this the girl taking you Ramallah?"

"Yes, sir. She is my friend," Rafi responded, holding up his passport. Americans so respected these soldiers, as if they were their own brothers, fighting great wars. Always "sir" from Raf when they met a soldier on the street, or when he insisted they give one a lift between Tel Aviv and Jerusalem.

"She force you go there?" the soldier asked. "She force?"

Nafiza bit her tongue. Her brother and cousins would call these soldiers "the working-class boys." They would rant, "How could we be under the thumb of these working-class boys?"

Rafi's eyes bugged. "Force me? God no!"

Both soldiers looked at her now, eyes saying, "Bitch." Then in Hebrew, the bearded one said to the other, "Search the car, yeah?"

Nafiza wanted to tell the soldiers that Raf was a writer, that he could make them look foolish in the papers if there was an unnecessary incident. She almost spoke, even though she knew that her voice would pierce at their pride and require even more punkish play. She almost yearned for an incident, shocking herself with bile. She felt like she had almost wanted this altercation to happen, just so she could have a fight.

The bearded soldier pushed away from the window, saying to the other, "She's a Palestinian whore. She wants to suck Jew cock because her own kind stink. But she's going American Jew, yeah? No Israeli man for her. She knows how we'd do her."

"Ofra! You crazy?" The dark one admonished in quick Hebrew. "You're going too far!"

"Fuck you!"

"That's right-wing shit. Don't go that far."

The dark soldier has saved us all, Nafiza thought, her heart pounding, her throat full. *He is saving us all. From me. I'm going to kill them!*

"You can pass," the soldier said, waving his arm at her. "Go on."

Nafiza pulled forward slowly. In the rearview mirror, she saw him shaking his head at his companion as he lit a cigarette.

Rafi, for a few seconds, had the sense to say or ask nothing, silenced by his own thoughts. Nafiza breathed deeply, returning to calm in the quick way she had learned early in life.

"What did they say?" Rafi finally asked, putting his passport back in his jacket pocket.

"Keep your passport out for the Palestinian checkpoint," she said.

It was just ahead, the cars in front of her accelerating for about fifty yards, then braking. She went into second gear, forcing the clutch badly, then back to first, ambling behind a line of Toyotas, Cortinas, and an old American pickup truck. Guiding the car, Nafiza felt both a seething and a serenity—a serenity that often scared her because in it she saw most clearly her visions of revenge and death.

"What were those assholes saying to you?" Rafi insisted.

"Just being Israeli men," she responded, eyes ahead.

"You don't let it get to you," he sighed, touching her hand which grasped the gearshift. "You're something. The new breed of Palestinian. So advanced. You're the future of peace."

She pulled her hand away, scratched her cheek. He noticed the rejection but did not push at her. Recovering his hand, he turned again to his pages.

"I've improved some of the first section of the poem," Rafi said.

Nafiza looked up at the cloudless blue sky, pulling sunglasses out of her fanny pack and putting them on. "Read me the first lines," she invited.

Nafiza listened, hearing a new word here or there. The poem

was such a naive thing, and not good poetry she thought, the production of a biochemist's mind, healing from emotional pain back home, and trying, so hard, to make sense. When they reached the gate, the Palestinian soldiers made them step out of the car for inspection. Nafiza tried to keep the lines of poetry in her mind, to take her to a place where poetry wasn't mainly the angry kind she read from her own people.

The Palestinians were suspicious of the American but not overtly aggressive. When the search was complete, she and Rafi started back out into traffic. He read more of the words he cared so much about, starting again with his title and a short paragraph he had revised many times already, as if it were part of the poem.

"*Making Peace with the Muslims*, a poem by Raf Horowitz, written while studying an Ottoman miniature painted on cow bone, from Southern Turkey, that sits in a home in Jerusalem, shared by an Israeli, a Palestinian, and an American. May poetry heal the world . . .

> *I see young warriors at their games,*
> *hand painted on bone like blood, and*
> *a Sultan's busy courtyard, circa 1530,*
> *spectators on the balcony,*
> *peasants on the street who watch men on horseback*
> *jab their lances at each other.*
> *I know the Sultan knew what we still know:*
> *boys' blood will spill, so let it spill not in war*
> *but in a circle of watchers on a holiday afternoon.*
> *Ramadan bread, shining*
> *with butter and smelling of sesame,*
> *bakes in the bakery nearby,*
> *beggars' odorous underarms, manure of horse carts,*
> *aromas of earth give way to fragrances*

of perfume from concubines,
and all fragrances give way to the maiden's,
the Sultan's daughter,
sweet black-veiled girl,
offered to the victor."

"You cut out some of the courtyard description," Nafiza commented, taking the car up to sixty kilometers per hour behind a truck.

"To make it tighter. I'm thinking about sending it to *The New Yorker* one day soon. I'm thinking bigger now than just one of the small university magazines."

He had told her a great deal about some sort of hierarchy of literary journals in America. It made little sense to her on its own, though she recognized the peculiar and necessary aggression of pecking orders. Rafi continued reading:

"I am looking at a scene on an Ottoman miniature
here in this Israeli home, so like one I saw years ago
in Diyarbakir, southeastern Turkey, a place
swollen, like Jerusalem, with a violent past.
Around me that day, dirty children in jeans
swarmed the donkey carts and food sellers,
dark-eyed men in shalvar fingered
their beads, their women shy, and cats
picked scraps from the garbage cans.
The Tigris was muddy, the buses stenched
with lamb's blood, the maniacal driver
flailed his wheeled lance at pedestrians—
in the jam-packed bus, a young Turk
admired my girlfriend's thigh, and beggars
held out brown, wizened, earth-bound hands."

Change a thing or two, and he could have been writing about her own West Bank, Nafiza had told him when she first heard the poem. He bent to his page, reading, soothing himself and soothing her. Nafiza smiled behind her sunglasses as she passed a donkey, women completely covered in *abaya*, muddy streets, dirty children, a skinny cat, an overcrowded bus.

Look up! she wanted to say to him. *Now we are entering my homeland.* But he enjoyed his reading:

> "*Turkey, home of my blood memory, toppler*
> *of great golden Byzantium, shudderer*
> *of Vienna's gates, your Ottomans stuffed*
> *my grandfather, an old proud Armenian,*
> *alive into an open mass grave in 1916;*
> *all your pride could not have dreamed*
> *your great past, how you would thrive*
> *at my expense, crow my black sorrow.*
> *For years I have tried to hate you,*
> *have walked your streets and the streets*
> *of all the black-turbaned lands—*
> *Damascus, Baghdad, Tehran, Cairo, Arabia,*
> *the West Bank where the boys flail out . . .*"

"Finally, today," Nafiza interrupted, "you'll be accurate about that."

Rafi grinned sheepishly. "Now I'll have been to *two* out of the six."

He had lived in Turkey for a year, and had been to Riyadh, but not to any of the other cities. Poetic license. His great-grandfather, an Armenian already in America by 1916, had told him about a cousin murdered and then dumped in a mass grave. More poetic license.

Gadi had been right—his distant cousin Rafi should have written it to be more about Jews, Arabs, Palestine, Israel. But Rafi did not really know this land, insisting on writing about Israel and Palestine in this allegorical way, with Turkey as the backdrop. Was this his escape from reality, his way of managing his own disappointment? More than once he'd said sadly to her, "What if there can't ever be real peace here in Palestine, Nafiza? What if Islam and Judaism are doomed to always fight?"

He had a big heart, this American. Would her parents see it? Probably. Her father was a secondary-school teacher and her mother a volunteer at the school infirmary. Would her brother and her cousins, their fists so full of rage these days? No. Now, after five weeks here, Rafi was finally entering the West Bank, finally seeing Palestinians beyond Jerusalem's old city. How many times, back in Jerusalem or in Tel Aviv or at Yaddo, he'd exclaimed, "I can't wait to actually meet a Palestinian family!"

Maybe he'd throw the whole poem out. Though Nafiza had the strange feeling that if he did, he'd become terribly lonely and depressed, and she would discover that she herself, in fact, had little impact on this big man's grief or happiness, certainly less than did his poetry. And it would sadden her too because he had rewritten the next part in the last weeks to include his feelings for her. How strange, she thought, listening to him read, that she could really care so much for this American who had lived so unheroic a life, a gangly, chatty man locked in laboratories, imagining himself something bigger, the taming—or perhaps just a bare cognizance—of Islam's secrets becoming his new mission in life. Could she love someone who was not cynical? She had never really tried.

> "... I have walked with my coat tight and a gun
> in my pocket and a knife in my belt,

for years I have put my ass out to you, oppressors . . .
But always I return to your courtyards,
always my eye rises there to your veiled
daughter, her tearless eyes, her jeweled
hand. Always I yearn to love her.
On Cinnah Caddesi, on Ziya Gokalp
where bus exhaust like black steam
scrapes my eyes to coal-dust tears;
in Erzurum where the Kurdish man
drives us to Ararat in his dying pickup,
his three wives and seventeen children in back;
in Bodrum, where the village elder
lies murdered by a pimp and his whore;
in Diyarbakir, dirty loving Diyarbakir,
where the Ottoman miniature sat dusty
on a rickety shelf in Ihsan Bey's shop,
as in Jerusalem, in a messy house of graduate students—
I reached for your dark daughter, I reached up
my long arm like a long branch of a linden tree
till my tired arm ached, a warrior's arm
after the victory, his mailed fist out
for the sweet fingers of the Sultan's daughter—
I reached up and I reached her down
while the unemployed tea-drinking men
all watched me. I counted out the Lira,
I let Ihsan Bey wrap the picture in cloth,
I smelled Ramadan bread from a bakery nearby,
shining with butter and speckled with sesame.
And when I left the shop and walked out
to the streets swarmed by children,
I felt the Ottoman miniature warm
in my hand, I felt the girl on my arm,

she was Mother Islam, who loved me,
every day she taught me to forgive,
for she had waited out all the centuries,
she was dark, and I was lonely to love her
and she knew pain, and she reached for me."

*   *   *

A car horn blasted outside the open window of the small house in the Beitunia district of Ramallah. A dusty heat touched everyone, and a wayward horsefly shot up near the ceiling. Here in the little sitting room, just adjacent to the dining nook, there was still the smell of coriander, thyme, and mint, all grown by Mama in the ten-foot-long garden outside her bedroom.

Nafiza had eaten little of the filleted beef, served in yogurt over rice. Her mother had called her the night before to talk over the menu, and to wonder aloud if it was a good idea to bring "this young Rafi from America" to the house, especially since intifada cousins Hamit and Ali insisted on coming over to meet him. "Coriander beef," Mama had finally decided. "A compromise between Palestinian and American food."

Sitting with her family now, Nafiza suddenly remembered herself and her brother years ago, standing in the camp between the outhouse and a barbed-wire fence, watching a group of Western doctors and nurses walk past. At nine years old, Nafiza's eye had stuck on one of the nurses who was plump, like Mama, and walked slowly, with good posture, her eyes focused directly in front of her, her stride purposeful. Nafiza remembered a near worship of the woman, and now could think of no reason why, except the resemblance to Mama.

Rafi read to the family as Papa scrutinized him with a tea glass in his hand. Papa was a scientist, a wise man whose wisdom came from careful observation and his Islam. Papa and Nafiza's brother, Ibish, were just completing their *zuhr*, the noon prayer, when she and Rafi had arrived today. Rafi had been touched with awe, or at least respect, and affected her with bare sentimentality.

Now, Rafi's poem read, Mama set her tea glass down and looked shocked by both the love in Rafi's poem and the confusion it would create.

Ibish said, "Interesting," puffing a Turkish Camel.

Hamit and Ali, teenagers, seemed to perennially seethe, both smoking Camels as well.

There were seven people today in the crowded sitting room. Turkish carpets, a taste acquired soon after they left the camps for a return to their family home in Ramallah, filled every inch of the hardwood floor. Here, in the north side of the room, the Western furniture, which had changed little since Nafiza and Ibish had grown up, was all browns and dark greens, kind to the eye for what they could afford. The room's other half was completely Palestinian—no chairs, a picture of Arafat on the wall, cushions covered with tight-woven sheaves, floor mats in both Arab and Turkish designs. Nafiza noticed a new cushion there since she'd been home last week for the weekly family meal ("Can't I please come, Nafiza!" Rafi had begged every time).

As she watched Rafi, she thought he had been intimidated since their arrival. Was he happy to be here?

"What do you study?" Papa had asked Rafi politely during dinner.

"The female endocrine system," Rafi had answered.

"Is San Francisco pretty?" Mama had asked.

Rafi's descriptions made it sound glorious.

"Why did you come here?" Ibish asked, a veiled way of digging in. Like Rafi, he wore a blue jacket, but one more discolored from the hours riding his bike in dust toward his mechanic's job at the other end of Ramallah.

"To this house?" Rafi had asked.

Ibish smiled and said, "To Palestine, I meant."

"To be a pilgrim," Rafi had answered, his mind obviously flickering behind his eyes as he noticed, over and over in the last hour, how no one referred to this place as Israel. He told them about dropping through mist out of the sky and he talked of hoping to find a new way of being here—his former relationship gone, his love of his biochemistry gone, his need to write poetry revived.

It was Mama who asked if he could recite some of his poetry for everyone. Mama so held things together here that even the surly look from Hamit, behind his smoke, might not touch Rafi.

Guided by his wife's force, Papa encouraged politely, "Do you memorize your poetry?"

Rafi laughed and said, "No. I wish I did. But I have a poem in the car."

Ibish volunteered to go get the manila file Rafi kept the pages in. Nafiza watched, almost shocked, as Rafi let Ibish go for his valuable poems. Even in her four years of education among Israelis, she had never trusted another person, outside her known relations, to handle something valuable to her.

As Ibish left the room, Ali said in Arabic, "You are digging in the bottom of the pit for this guy, Nafiza. You could do better with a boy from Moustaribine."

His visceral placement of Rafi below even a member of the Israeli underground forces who disguised themselves as Arabs brought not hurt but a sarcastic smile to Nafiza's face.

Before she could retort, Mama said, "We will speak English, and we will be polite. If you cannot do that, my husband will ask you to leave, cousins."

Invoking Papa among his own blood kin was smart, and perhaps even expected by Ali and Hamit, the more silent, sullen one. Though Nafiza had expected them to be here today, and though she had warned Rafi to just try to get them out of his mind—"They don't speak much English, so you won't hear from them much"—she wished they had not bothered to come. She felt sadness for her mother who, trapped by family convention, could not really turn them away.

"Mr. abu-Hussein," Rafi said to Papa, pretending he had not sensed the invective from the two teenagers, "what do you think is the key to helping Israel and Palestine find peace now that we are nearly in a new millennium?"

Papa sat back in his chair, looking toward the picture of Arafat, responding immediately as if he had just been waiting for political conversation. "I believe, until one admits one's weaknesses, one cannot advance. One's future is in honesty about one's weaknesses."

Papa carefully brushed the front of his vest with an open palm. He had greased his hair back today, and though a short, plump man, he, like Mama, was handsome. His jaw sat firmly below large lips and well-spread eyes on a smooth brown face, which looked older than his fifty-one years.

"You see, Mr. Horowitz, Palestinians have been forced to meet their own weaknesses. Israel has not yet. When it does, it will understand how to compromise with us. I believe this."

Ibish returned, asking, "Are these the papers?"

"Thank you." Rafi grinned, standing up so that he towered over the smaller Ibish. He started to explain the poem, how he had started this version that night at Gadi's, seeing the Ottoman miniature in the house, remembering his time in Turkey when he was a tourist years ago, especially his time in Diyarbakir, thinking about how the Ottomans had been a conquering force like Israel was now. He talked about how in Turkey, where Europe and Asia met, he had thought peace between East and West possible. He talked about how he had wanted to get out of biochemistry for some time, maybe join the Peace Corps. He talked about how he hoped that in Israel—"I mean, Palestine," he added apologetically—he would get his poetic gifts back, because they were what he needed now. And he mentioned, with a wry look, "There's a girl in this poem, a wonderful girl. She crept in somehow." He winked at Nafiza who, suddenly a child of convention, bowed her head and flushed.

And then he read the poem, ending it with lines new to her, written only in the last few days and kept as a surprise for the visit home to her parents.

> *And I said to her, I have a sweet love to give*
> *that I hold like this Ottoman miniature.*
> *I give it to you, my beautiful dark girl,*
> *I release this love, hand-crafted on delicate bone.*
> *Will you take up this priceless piece*
> *in your playful hands?*
> *I will wait for you, at a cliffside, or a hard wall,*
> *or just walking past David's tomb one day in Jerusalem,*
> *wait until you shatter this bone on rock,*
> *a gift now yours, my dear,*
> *to use as you please, perhaps to build the heart*
> *or simply to destroy the delicate cruelties of the past.*

Nafiza, remembering Rafi's hidden hurt after Gadi's critique, quickly thought to begin a game her father and brother loved—the game of argument. She smiled at Rafi, so he would know her appreciation of his gift, then she said, "It seems to me you men always need two lovers, one your friend, and one the daughter of your enemy."

Rafi looked quizzical and Papa leaned back a little, attentive.

"Aren't men," Nafiza said to her mother, "always fighting battles their grandfathers should have won?"

"Indeed. Yes." Mama seemed to enjoy her daughter's piquant accuracy. To protect her husband's social pride, she always deferred to him, and even to Ibish, on the street, near the mosque, or anywhere that did not involve intimate relations. But from as early as Nafiza could remember, even in the camps, when Mama was among her own family, she liked a soft critique of the male way of being.

Rafi said, "Nafiza, you've just said in a few words what it took me a whole poem to say."

Hamit leapt in, speaking furious Arabic. "There can be no peace here until the right of return is every Palestinian's right. Tell him that. Translate that. No Palestinian shall give up his family's ancestral home or location. Every Palestinian must be given back his home taken by the Israelis in all of our towns. Tell him that. He should put that in his poem."

There was a silence, Ali putting out his cigarette in a white ashtray.

"Translate that!" Hamit insisted to Nafiza, who had been translating, along with her brother, the rest of the conversation and the poem.

Nafiza looked to her mother, who looked at Hamit angrily. Papa took hold of the situation by performing the translation himself.

Hamit stood up, a boy-man, just eighteen, muscular in his jeans and brown T-shirt, just under six feet tall. "What do you think, American?" he challenged in Arabic.

Mama was about to speak, but Papa lifted his hand. He seemed to say, "Let the young man speak, let him ask his questions, receive his answers, then he will be satisfied and calm down."

Rafi answered, looking up at the younger man. "I don't know what to think. I don't know how thousands of Israelis can move out of their homes and give them back to Palestinians. But I don't know how they can't. I don't know. Just like I'm sure you do, I just hope for peace. Soon. I hope I can do my part for peace."

The last thing Hamit wanted was peace, Nafiza knew. Rafi wanted it like a poet wants it—for its beauty, not its necessity.

Do I want it? Nafiza wondered.

She'd gone to Hebrew University, the first in her family to try to cross over, an object of both respect and disgust in her own Palestinian world. To many here in Ramallah, she had become a kind of tourist. Sometimes she wanted to be Hamit and Ali, throwing stones. Other times, she wanted to be Anwar Sadat, sewing peace. My, my, she thought, Rafi's poem does have a certain power to air out some windows.

"Peace, as things stand now, is impossible," Nafiza said, both in English and Arabic, trying to release herself from ambivalence to some sort of power. "Most Jews at Hebrew University aren't even sure they want it. I think peace is an impossible task."

Papa frowned. "I can't accept that, as long as the impossibility of the task inspires us. Impossibility must not defeat us, not make us cynics."

Nafiza nodded automatic agreement, realizing that for a split second she really admired Hamit's youthful anger more than her father's solidity or Rafi's relative worthlessness in the real battle going on around him.

"There is a story," Papa said to Rafi. "A Palestinian, a very godly man, is in prison. There is no way to get the key to the locks in order to free himself. One day a prayer carpet is thrown into his cell. He spreads it five times a day, for many months, performing his prayers. He begins to notice that in the carpet is now the outline where his head had been so many times. Furthermore, he notices that the outline of his head is the exact design of the locks mechanism in his cell door. Now, with only the simplest of metal slivers from a bedspring, he can unlock the door."

Nafiza saw disgust on Hamit and Ali's faces. She saw Ibish drop his head, a little in shame of his own father's hopefulness. Only because of conventions of respect for their uncle did the teenagers not cry out in disgust. Religious youth, yes, but more political militants than prayerful men, they did not like religion to be used as a calming influence.

Mama stood up to take the tea tray to the kitchen. "Come, Nafiza," she said. "We'll clean up."

The men stood respectfully.

Ali picked up his cigarettes, pocketing them in his gray jacket pocket. "We will go, Uncle," he said to Papa.

Rafi shook each boy's hand politely. Both Hamit and Ali kept their eyes toward Ibish and Papa as they shook Rafi's hand. Rafi seemed to choose not to notice the slight, retaining a smile.

Nafiza followed her mother to the dual-sided porcelain sink, scrubbed to shiny whiteness every day.

"Take young Rafi out for some air," Mama said, taking the dessert plates from Nafiza. "He is well-meaning. Show him our city."

Nafiza hugged her mother's shoulders. "Thank you for letting him come. He was desperate to come. Things went okay today, I think."

As well as they could go, she thought, but hardly okay.

"He likes you," Mama said, putting on her rubber gloves.

"He is my Romeo, I'm his Juliet. I like him, but I know it is impossible between us."

"You cannot have marriage or children together," Mama agreed. "But he seems very nice."

Nafiza felt certainties here in her family's home. "We could not live here in Palestine or in Israel. And I don't want to go to America."

Mama looked into her daughter's eyes. Nafiza organized dishes in the drainer, avoiding her mother's eyes as the older woman contemplated for a moment just how far things had gone.

"No," Mama agreed simply, eyes back to the dishes. "You cannot leave here for the USA."

For a moment there was only the clink of dessert dishes and silverware, the sound of water running from the tap, and silent thoughts. Then Rafi laughed loudly in the other room.

"Go," Mama said. "Let me finish alone."

Nafiza kissed her and turned to find the men again.

"Ibish, I think I get that joke," Rafi was saying.

The men were standing, Rafi trying to smoke a cigarette with her father and brother, a cloud of smoke around them all. He wanted to hold Nafiza's hand as she came next to him and suggested they walk. She looked into her father's eyes, smiling, avoiding Rafi's hand, thankful to be returned in these few moments to the knowledge, always present though often supplanted over the last weeks by pleasure, that she was not Rafi's to keep, nor he hers.

When they walked out the front door a few minutes later, past Mama's white lattice draped in purple bougainvillea and into the street, Rafi commented, "No sidewalks here either." Every few days he mentioned this difference from America. America must be filled with sidewalks to hear him tell it.

An old man with a donkey and cart of plastic containers had set up shop across the street, selling to Mrs. Al-Khalil, who waved to Nafiza while looking Rafi over. The street, so familiar to her, brought questions from Rafi. He wondered if he could go into the mosque that stood like a large ship before them. Its single spire, ornamented at the top, was the tallest thing around. She dissuaded him. She also suggested they not hold hands, which he understood.

He had shoved his poem in his inside jacket pocket. Now they turned the corner onto Nagil Avenue, Nafiza chatting a moment here or there with someone she knew, introducing her friend from America. Rafi asked questions about houses, people, street names. He seemed amazed to learn that so many of the people here had been raised or lived in camps. Rafi also remarked, when a Palestinian soldier passed, how calm things seemed, all and all. He had not really expected to see violence today—as Nafiza assured him he wouldn't—but he confessed to feeling a visceral fear that she might be wrong.

"I'm the foreigner here," he said, "that's for sure."

Palestinian men, some in traditional headwear, walked by Rafi with glaring eyes. Not a single one stopped to talk to this stranger, or to Nafiza. On Nagil, Rafi thought he saw Ali up ahead, pointing to a young man walking in a blue windbreaker with three other teen boys. They were entering the market area whose smell of hay, vegetables, and horse manure already rose in Nafiza's nostrils. Rafi wanted to say hello to an old woman selling potatoes, Mrs. Saidi. The old woman kissed Nafiza and shook Rafi's hand, trying to chat with him in broken English.

Leaving her stall, Rafi cried, "I love these smells!"

He saw a girl whose face and hands had been colored in reddish henna. She was perhaps nine or ten, walking right up to this skinny tower of an American. In newly learned, broken

English, she told him she had seen *Scooby-Doo* on the television. He laughed loudly, and people turned to look, but only for a moment. He may or may not have been a Jew, but everyone knew that he was surely an American. Americans were so obvious. In total, they were a frightening mass of money and power. But as individuals, they were all the same tourist.

As Rafi bought a pear from Mr. abu-Massam—whose eyes Nafiza avoided, for she knew he would judge her companionship openly, with words, if she gave him a chance—Nafiza thought silently how strong she felt as she walked with this stranger among her own people. She had thought she would be overwhelmed by stares, judgments, shame. She had not trusted, she realized now, as Rafi offered the first bite, had not trusted herself to be strong and individual, had not trusted her own people to have matured beyond the world of the camps.

And now, watching the pear's saliva-like bead of liquid cling to Rafi's lower lip along his beard, watching his eyes taking her in with wonder and admiration, envisioning herself running a hand through his hair, right here, on the street—her yearning and bravery closeted for hours, but now rising—she felt a sweet urge to guide him behind the market, to a spot behind the smelly garbage pile, where she could give him a kiss.

"Come with me," Nafiza whispered, taking his hand.

"Where?"

"That alley. I'll show you lots of smells!" she laughed. "And also, a kiss." She was surprised to feel such a stirring in her loins. "I want you!"

They walked behind the last open stall, vacant today, past a woodpile and toward twin piles of garbage, mainly vegetable leavings and rotting wood.

"Jesus, the smell!" He held his nose in an exaggerated way.

"Not a lot of people come back here," Nafiza said.

There were buildings on each side of them, one a two-story apartment building and the other a one-story, boxlike house. Both, like all the buildings around, were an off-white, paint peeling down to the gray concrete.

"This is like making love in my parents' house." Rafi grinned as Nafiza leaned against a wall, her simple dress—into which her mother had asked her to change—caressing her skin like a closed-in cage. Nafiza could not ever imagine even necking in her parents' house. She had never even kissed a boy here in Ramallah. Perhaps that was why she felt such desire now.

"God, you're beautiful!" Rafi declared, looking down at her.

Then, it was as if, for a split second, time exploded. Rafi was hit on the back of the head, his eyes widening in shock, his head smashing forward just over her right shoulder, into the wall. She heard a dull crack, and she screamed into his body.

Two boys—faces hidden in cloth—ran at her. One held a rock. The other had just thrown his. One of the boys hissed at her to shut up, fierceness in his eyes. He hit Rafi's head with his jagged rock, blood spurting. Nafiza was now trapped between Rafi and the wall, her face splattered by thick red blood. She closed her eyes, shut her mouth instinctively, groaning. She was going to be beaten. She wanted to scream, she tried to scream, but a hand came across her mouth. Her hands went up to push at the boy who smelled of cologne. Hamit and Ali had sent them. It must be. But who were they? Both boys held her now, one pinning her neck with his arm and crushing her body against the wall, the other holding her hair back viciously. They were not speaking, hiding in silence. She must know them. Rafi lay on the ground, unconscious.

She bit the hand, drawing blood. The boy cried out, then hit her. She fell, her back skidding against the wall. Flailing her arms, she tried to stop her skid. Her right thigh hit Rafi's shoulder, then she hit her head on the cement next to him. For a second, she was unconscious from the blow. One of the boys kicked her in the ribs. The other kicked Rafi. Her face was covered in blood, and she felt a terrible pain and an ooze above her temple and in her hair at the back of her head. Her hands tried to move to her head, her ribs. A man's voice, shouting, stopped the boys suddenly. They ran. Was it Mr. Fallat running over? Now a woman's voice too. And there was the terrible stench of rot, of blood, and still the boy's cologne.

"It is Nafiza Thura!" Mr. Fallat cried. Now more voices, people, hands.

"Rafi!" Nafiza cried. A handkerchief was suddenly in her hand as she tried to remove blood from her eyes.

A woman's voice said, "Look. The American."

A young man's voice said, "She should not have brought him here."

Hands helped her up.

"Go get abu-Hussein and Ibish," a man ordered. Nafiza's eyes, now clouded not by blood but some kind of triple image, saw outlines of Mr. Masima, a salesman, in front of her.

"The American is breathing," someone said.

Nafiza heard papers being collected before she turned to see Mrs. Masima collecting Rafi's poem. Now Rafi uttered a groan.

"I will get my car," Mr. Masima rose up and then ran. The clinic was only blocks away.

"Nafiza?" Rafi groaned. His face was covered in blood, his eyes finding her as he wiped at them. A man kneeled next to him, trying to help, his own handkerchief red with Rafi's blood. Rafi tried to reach for Nafiza, but by the aid of all the hands around him, it was as if he were being restrained from her.

"There were two boys," Nafiza said.

How terribly she wanted to cry, "Go find Hamit and Ali!

They'll know about it!" but she said nothing. No one here, even the first witnesses present, would say anything to catch the culprits. Even if she spoke up, the Palestinian police would look at her grimly, "He is a Jew, you are Palestinian. Your cousins are Palestinian. Finished."

What would Rafi do? What would he tell the police? Now Rafi was trying to grasp his papers, still on his knees, as two women helped Nafiza to stand.

"Why did you bring him here?" one asked, not maliciously, not even in anger, just reserving in her voice that right any onlooker enjoyed, to speak the obvious.

With a concussed glaze in his eyes, Rafi was murmuring something about Sheri, then about his poem. He dropped the bloody file and papers, and a man helped him gather them. Blood dripped off Rafi's beard.

"Nafiza!" Papa's voice, breathless, came through the small crowd.

Nafiza was upright now, holding her head, the figures and shadows in her eyes lessening toward one vision. Even in the camps, even in towns always in the thick of a war, Nafiza had not herself been hurt this way since childhood.

"Papa!" she cried.

Ibish took her arm as Papa held her. Mama ran up behind, equally breathless, and now wailing at the sight of her bloodied daughter.

* * *

It was the brightest and sunniest of days when Rafi got on the airplane. Not only did the sky hold its glaring blue cloudlessly, but an almost blinding whiteness thickened in Nafiza's eyes as she watched the El-Al jet take off with Raf Horowitz.

"He seems okay," Gadi said matter-of-factly, smoke from his cigarette snaking out his half-open window.

In the two weeks since "the incident," Nafiza had spent most of the time in Ramallah, her professors quite understanding. Nafiza's sexual, even romantic desire for the American had disappeared almost completely. When Gadi called her with the exact details of Rafi's flight, she knew she must have the courage to face him, to see him off. For days after the incident, he had tried to get her to tell the police who the boys were, suspecting rightfully that if she wanted to, she could be helpful. She insisted she knew nothing. He had turned away from her, and as he turned, leaving any possible love to die, she saw that he was weeping.

In the airport terminal, there had been mainly silence between them. Gadi read a newspaper. Raf gave a clean copy of his poem to her, having kept the bloody one for himself or thrown it away; she did not ask. She accepted the poem as a part of the surreal life she had led for over a month.

Handing it to her, Raf said, as if he had practiced the words, "I don't know how I thought I could make peace with the Muslims when even you, a Muslim, have not."

Looking at his head bandaged in white, almost like a turban, Nafiza thought for a second that she glimpsed the complete pattern of the world. But she had no words for it. She wondered what Raf Horowitz would do after he went back to America, how he would live, whom he would love. He said he was going to join the Peace Corps. She thought he probably would. He could not make a living writing poetry.

She took the poem and thanked him. Now, watching from the car as his plane became a dot in the sky, she opened his envelope, noticing a handwritten note with the poem. She read it aloud to Gadi.

Nafiza, I hope you will never give up on peace. Maybe words don't have the power that the action of blood has, but we must still dream that peace is possible.

Gadi laughed. "Making peace with the Muslims? The greatest minds in Israel haven't done it, and that *nebbisher* American thought he could."

"I wish I could love him for the effort," Nafiza said. "The sheer human effort. He was like someone from another time." But she couldn't. In her experience, momentous efforts, if unrequited or disavowed, always led to greater pain for everyone.

Gadi grunted, starting the car. Nafiza closed her eyes, her head still aching after two weeks, her hand going to the wound at her right temple and the bandage. She wished she could tell Gadi, her family, even Raf Horowitz—who would perhaps best understand—that she had been utterly ashamed of her cousins and the brutal boys they enlisted, ashamed that not only she herself, but her brother, mother, and father too, had avoided hinting any truth to the authorities; and yet that also, within her anger and shame, was an almost desperate pride in her cousins, in the boys, in her people, and even in herself. No one, she suspected, truly knew her rage. No one knew that for a second, while watching them hit Raf, her ambivalence had stretched so far as to accept, without regret, that he might be dead.

Nafiza opened her eyes. The moving car gave her a rhythm in which to breathe, to swallow, to breathe again. She leaned forward against the dashboard.

"You okay?" Gadi asked.

"I'm fine."

She leaned back. Breathing deeply felt good, and she opened the window all the way. Gadi smashed out his cigarette in the ashtray.

Gadi always drove fast. Now they passed a rusted tank, half buried in sand. A few moments later, they passed three men at the side of the road on their knees in *Salat*. Just beyond them, a family stepped out of a car.

Nafiza lifted her eyes toward the blue-white sky, following its flat magnificence toward the sea. She wondered over America, but for only a second, trying instead to return to herself completely. She was a Palestinian girl who had enough trouble just getting a degree in economics at a Jewish university. She should bid the high heights and lofty thoughts goodbye as she accepted that Raf's plane was completely gone. She should return her thoughts to the textbooks she had not opened in two weeks, the tests she had not taken, and her real work—to survive in both Israel and in Palestine, neither escaping from nor surrendering to either world.

"I'll be okay," she said to Gadi, who nodded, and lit another cigarette, offering one to her.

She had stopped smoking since Raf disliked the smell of cigarettes, but now she took a long draught of the sweet smoke and leaned her head back, letting the hot breeze off the desert touch her lips, her cheeks, her eyelids. She let herself linger in its whoosh of sound, the dusty smell, and the soft windy fingers as if they might, thick with the power of many old gods and that ancient promise of meaning, heal her wounds.

irina's lullaby

"She's so restless she'll *never* sleep," Elaine sighed as she dropped next to her aunt Beatrice on the velvet-covered couch with three-month-old Irina in her arms.

"I'll take her if you like," Ursula offered, reaching across the little end table from the easy chair. Ursula, an acting teacher from Paris, was just under sixty, which made her the youngest of this elderly Saturday evening crowd at Château Benoît, Aunt Beatrice's huge, five-story, twelve-bedroom family home in Evreaux. They had begun to arrive the previous evening for a weekend of horseback riding, country walks, festive meals—Aunt Beatrice made a game hen with mustard sauce that everyone loved—and to fuss over Elaine's new baby, mother and daughter having just arrived from Algiers.

Elaine passed the baby over to the delighted Ursula, who wore her blonde pulled back into a chignon. Her face was still smooth and her biceps well-defined—Ursula was one of those older middle-aged women who lifted weights—her eyes blue with a red tint from the glow of the fireplace, her brown slacks creased, and her blouse a creamy white.

"I'm Atlas and I've shrugged," Elaine smiled gratefully.

Already, in the few seconds that she'd been held by Ursula, Irina had mellowed. Once out of her mother's arms, she always mellowed. Why was it, Elaine thought, Irina's father, Jean-Pierre Salim Zanoun, had the same magic with the baby?

For half an hour Elaine had wandered in the oak-paneled dining room, amid the two-hundred-year-old chairs and table, along

the ancient Persian carpets, murmuring to Irina, showing her ancestral portraits on the walls, feeding her from her breast, trying
to calm her down. Irina's nappies were dry, and her eyes glassy
with exhaustion, but she fussed to be brought to *baba*—though
Salim, still in Algiers, would not arrive until next week—or back
out to sweet but frumpy Aunt Beatrice, elegant but casual Ursula,
Beatrice's beer-bellied American boyfriend, Bert, almost seventy,
and the old Scottish couple, Ivy and Jim, whom Aunt Beatrice
had met while doing her Friday shopping in Evreux, on her way
out here from Paris. She brought these "new friends" out with her
to Château Benoît for the weekend, "because they just seemed
so nice." Beatrice had always been like that—generous, curious,
welcoming to everyone. Despite her dislike, during Elaine's teen
years, of some of her boyfriends, Beatrice had never been ungra-
cious to any young man. She was an upper-class woman, but not
an elitist. Egalitarian to the core, she tried to see the best in everyone, and gave twenty percent of her annual income to charities,
most of them relating to youth and children.

Elaine watched everyone coo at Irina now. The baby had
quieted, trying to take in each human sound separately, until
they overwhelmed her. Ursula giggled at the touch of Irina's tiny
brown hand. Bert gave the baby a little wave. The old Scottish
couple sighed. One had to admit this was a relief, even though the
last thing Salim would want was his three-month-old daughter
to spend a lot of time here. When he arrived in a week, he'd see
how the old people swept little Irina up in all their soft wrinkles,
fed her sweets, interfered with her routines, criticized Elaine's
disciplines. And since she'd arrived in Paris on Thursday, Elaine
herself had had the feeling that something terrible was going to
happen: that Aunt Beatrice, who never raised children, would
drop Irina headfirst onto the sidewalk; or that Ursula would
wheel her, in the huge stroller Beatrice had bought, into the path

of a horse. If not that Elaine would inherit Château Benoît, one of the last family-owned manors of its kind in France, from Aunt Beatrice upon death; if not that she and Salim had already made and remade numerous condominium plans for Benoît's future (Salim so passionate—"When she dies, we'll turn that colonialist palace on its ear; we'll sell it, make a fortune on development, spend the money on the countries colonized"—he meant Algiers and Palestine); if not for a certain grudging love of Aunt Beatrice, Elaine would have stayed in Algiers. She would certainly not have come out to Benoît.

"I'm trapped," she wrote Salim on a postcard this morning. "Please come, save me soon from this huge museum in Normandie filled with its bunch of old mannequins." Salim truly disliked these people, but he had insisted she answer Aunt Beatrice's call to see the baby. "We must be intelligent," he said. He and his friends at the university already spoke of the good the inheritance would do. Aunt Beatrice knew nothing of the plan; if fact, she liked and trusted Salim, who had, on the one occasion they met—at the wedding— been polite to her.

"Don't worry—our stories will get the dear baby to sleep soon," Aunt Beatrice said, leaning in to run her finger along Irina's cheek. "We've been telling stories about your favorite subject, Elaine—the war."

"Not that," Elaine groaned. "It's a ghastly subject."

"I just learned something," Aunt Beatrice went on, as if she hadn't heard. "Ivy says that Glasgow and Belfast were both bombed in forty-four. Did you know that, Elaine? That the Luftwaffe bombing went that far north?"

Elaine shook her head. Elaine had been reading modern European history at the Sorbonne until she met Salim there, and then switched to contemporary Arab studies. Elaine had never been to Scotland, but she imagined all old Scotswomen looking like Ivy, eyes small, a whitish blue, lips overly lipsticked, hair completely white, up in a bun. Her husband, Jim, sat back in his chair, his legs straight out, his hands folded on his thin belly.

"Hey, Bea, tell the Scots *your* story of the Occupation," the Texan, Bert, said in his slow way. "It's a good story." In the ten years he'd been with Aunt Beatrice, he still sounded to Elaine like John Wayne. To Jim, he said, "This mansion was a Nazi headquarters."

Aunt Beatrice grinned. "As Bert's son once told me: 'Beatrice, you *did* the Occupation,' which, I believe, is like *doing* Europe. So American!"

"What can I say?" Bert raised his hands in a mea culpa.

Elaine had once had a crush on Bert's son, just five years ago, in fact, when she was seventeen, on a trip with Beatrice and Bert to America. That seemed so long ago, such another world, another world view. She had made out with Justin in his father's Oldsmobile Toronado, a huge hulk of a car. Justin had been passionate but, in the end, Elaine had held onto her virginity. When she came to know Salim, she knew that God—or Allah— had been looking out for her. She fell head-over-heels in love with Salim who, though a modern man, was a Muslim, and would have, in some strange way Muslim men had, feared her lack of virginity, and thus, probably some years into marriage, rejected her.

Now Ursula gave Irina to Ivy, who, herself a grandmother of six, yearned for a cuddle. As she rocked the baby, Ivy insisted that the "Occupation story" be told. That was all the encouragement Aunt Beatrice needed. She leaned forward a little, took a sip of wine, a fifteen-year-old Merlot, then began to describe how the Germans came rumbling down the long pebble driveway of Benoît, up to the huge oak front door, knocking politely; how they met three servants and Great-Grandmama, who spoke fluent German—she was part Bavarian; how, politely, they asked her and her staff to stay around as the soldiers moved through the house, taking it. They would like it very much, they said, if she looked after them. And so Grandmama became their servant, and Aunt Beatrice, who came out from Paris quite a bit as a child, often stayed with her, helping her. Beatrice recalled that Grandmama even flirted with the young German men like an old woman can do with soldiers far from their families, a motherly flirtation. Aunt Beatrice was too young to be looked at as anything but a girl.

Hoping her face betrayed nothing—not her disdainful boredom, nor her unexpected lack of boredom either—Elaine sat back into the couch, watching Irina's rapt eyes. Right now, they stared at bald Bert, his usual cowboy hat off indoors, his glasses incredibly thick, the firelight reflected in them, his hands, like Scottish Jim's, folded on his tummy, but his tummy, unlike the smaller man's, a huge mound. As Ivy sniffled, Irina's eyes moved up to her face; as Bert cleared his throat, her gaze shifted back over to him. Ursula reached for Irina, and Ivy returned the swaddled baby to her.

Elaine closed her eyes for a second, the firelight flickering in her after-vision. She tried to imagine herself as a grandmother. She wondered where Salim was now. At a meeting, probably. Would he ever have as much a passion for anyone as he did for the Arab identity and the support of Arab causes? To love him was to be compelled to love his passion—only under its shadow would he love a woman. Elaine knew it, yet she did feel loved.

"My father, mother, and brother were in Paris the whole time," Aunt Beatrice went on, "and Benoît somehow got by. This was all, of course, until the Gestapo came. These killers started coming late in the war, when they knew they were losing. Any local in their presence for too long was a reminder of defeat, so they mistreated everyone. Grandmama sent me back to Paris where it was safer. Imagine! I nearly didn't get there, for Gestapo identity checks and train checks and the like. To this day, I haven't set foot in Germany, as Ursula knows. Too many bad memories.

Irina suddenly kicked, jerkily and hard, against Ursula's arms. Ursula tried to calm her, but Elaine leaned in, offering to take her. Ursula handed the baby over, then settled back in her chair, legs crossed, hands tight in her lap. Elaine had suspected for some time that Ursula didn't like the Germany-bashings at Benoît, but her barely-wrinkled face—a polished actor's mask so accustomed to drama—showed polite interest, and she always sat through the same conversations, over and over again. Why?

"I'll never forget," Aunt Beatrice told them, her lips pursed, "the drive back out here with my father in forty-five. We knew nothing of what had gone on out here in the last months of the war, even after the Germans surrendered. I worried terribly over Grandmama and Benoît. A few days after everyone stopped being drunk with victory, Papa told me it was time to drive out to the castle. He told me I could come only if I promised to be a big girl. Grandmama might be dead, and the château destroyed.

"I'll never forget my pounding heart. The whole drive from Paris—pounding. I loved my grandmother more than anything. When we turned down the road from Conches, I was dizzy. I said a prayer and I closed my eyes very tight. When I opened them, we had turned along the outer drive. I saw five or six burned tanks in the garden. There were black burns on the grass, on the dirt, on the tree trunks. When we turned the last corner, I saw the manor. I'll never forget it. The door was crooked, windows broken, the iron gate bent, paint steamed and burned off. But it was there!

"We pulled up front, got out of the car, and then heard a scream . . . a scream like a combination of a pigeon cooing and a little girl squealing. My old Grandmama came running out!" Irina listened, eyes half closed toward sleep. Elaine found herself listening too, despite having heard it all before.

"Dogs barked somewhere in the distance. There was an old man digging around in the dirt near the caretaker's cottage. My Grandmama was hugging me. What a day it was. How alive we all were! How a part of everything! A remarkable day, more memorable than all the bad years of the war. Since then, I've been even more attached to this house. Elaine, when she gets it, will let her husband from a foreign land tear it down and build condos."

"No, no, Beatrice!" Elaine cried. How did she know?

Aunt Beatrice dismissed Elaine's shocked denial with a wave of her hand. "But I always see Benoît as it was on that day," she continued. "A survivor. Even if that does make me a Zionist-capitalist, or worse . . ." she lowered her voice, as if hiding from Elaine, ". . . an aristocrat, a colonialist." She let out an elderly lady's chortle.

How had her aunt known? Or was that just a test . . . a probing . . . to see if it was what Elaine actually planned? That might be what it was.

"Honey"—Bert set his large hand on her hand—"never be sorry for a tale with a happy ending."

Ivy held up her hand slightly. "Why, just the opposite! Celebrate it! I know it's hard to keep up châteaux these days. But yours has memories. Your story sends the mind back. I remember something I haven't thought about in years. May I tell you?"

"Of course," Aunt Beatrice responded, shifting her body in the sofa. Irina's eyes were nearly closed. Elaine rocked her gently. Aunt Beatrice, she noticed—always a little overweight, especially for her short stature—had been getting thinner over the last few years. Her evening clothes, a loose cotton shirt and pleated tan pants, fit her more loosely than years ago.

Ivy pulled a crumpled handkerchief out of her left jacket sleeve and wiped her nose. She had done this all evening, victim of some sort of sinus problem.

"It's when you said you felt really alive, that's what reminded me," she told them. "Sometimes a place can get inside you. A house, a garden, a road. You remember the shelter on Dumbarton, Jim?"

Her husband squinted at the memory. "Of course, you do. We were children. I was just a girl, just thinking of college, just a little younger than yourself, Elaine. I didn't know I would marry Jim then. We spent many nights down in that shelter, our Glasgow dungeon, too many to even pass remarks. But this one night, the bombs came down like rain. Like rain! We sat in the crowded wee shelter giving the Germans up and down the banks—'They'll get a whipping from our boys, they will, any day now,' all full of ourselves, and scared too.

"And there was this terrible man, ancient as can be, face like a wizened potato, sitting calm as you please right next to me. 'Oh aye,' he's going on, 'Oh aye, Glasgow's an open book to me'—he had a terrible highlands accent—'Would you like me to tell you, lass, what that bomb just took out? 'Twas the eastern rail. And that other 'twas the primary school.'

"Oh, he got into me something fierce. I told myself, he's a gray old man just takin' the mickey. Ha ha ha. No, I won't believe a word. But with bombs falling everywhere, the ground shaking, young mothers biting their nails, still as the dead, seeing their houses gone, and where might their husbands be right now—caught at work maybe? Who's to know what's possible and what's not? Hadn't the steel factory gone last week? Hadn't the boys' school gone the week before?

"I was getting beside myself. I wanted to yell at the old man, 'Stop now, just stop.' And maybe I'd just about found the courage to say it. But then comes the final straw, scares the wits out of me. 'That one near nicked the Queen's College,' he nodded. 'Next one's going there.' No, I thought. No, it couldn't. There was talk I could go to the Queen's, get a university degree the next year. Not many girls could make a go of it. But if the Germans took it out, I'd be no more than I ever was, a girl with no future. I prayed like a madwoman. What a terrible night."

Ivy paused, took a deep breath, dropped her tensed shoulders and replaced her handkerchief. Elaine's memory, like a path of images parallel to Ivy's, saw the Palestinian refugee camp Salim had taken her to on their honeymoon—he had insisted on a trip to Palestine, and he never called it Israel. Elaine saw the impoverished people with beaten eyes and knew there was a world of suffering she had not been able, until that moment, even to fully imagine. She was almost ashamed of her ignorance—she, a history student. These people were not history—they were the present.

"Then what do you think happened? Another set of bombs falling, then another, and a terrible tumbling all around, and what do you think the old fart comes out with? Aye, you guessed it: 'That's the Queen's College, lass, hit dead to rights. Won't be much of that left now.'

"I started weeping like a banshee. I cried out that it was the end of the world, and he thought I'd gone mad. Wasn't but five, ten minutes later the all-clear sounded, and me still sniffling. Everyone started up out of the shelter, anxious to see the damage. I let everyone go ahead of me. Mum was pressing me to come on. I was too scared to. Sometimes, nowadays, when I go through those airplane tunnels at the airport, I think I'm coming out of the shelters.

"Anyway, to tell you how it turned out, I came up out of the shelter, started walking down the street behind Mum and Dad, my head down like a scared wee bride, not daring to look up and see the Queen's towers gone. Dad knew why I was suffering. He came beside me and whispered, 'Ivy, raise your head now and look what God has done.' He nearly forced my head up, chin first. He pointed over the trees and into such a pretty blue sky, and I saw the towers standing there, clear as day, unharmed and untouched. I thought I was flying just then. I thought I was floating in the breeze. What a sweet, sweet day. Another happy ending, if ever there was one. And I went to the Queen's College, didn't I, Jim?"

Irina had completely relaxed. Elaine lay her baby's sleeping head in the crook of her right arm.

"She never lets me forget it," the Scottish man nodded, his face small, eyes close together, white hair greased back. "You know what we say up around Glasgow?" he asked. "We say, 'Squash a beetle and it'll rain.' That's what happened with the Germans."

Eyebrows were raised in polite incomprehension.

"Sure, it did," he explained. "That Versailles Treaty squashed the very life out of the Germans, and did not the rain come? It did indeed. A fierce rain at that."

"Ah, yes," Aunt Beatrice said. "I see what you mean."

"Jim's always coming out with things like that." Ivy chuckled. "Just give him a biscuit, and he'll be happy."

"Two, please." He grinned.

"Look at the baby," Aunt Beatrice whispered. Irina's eyelids fluttered as she slept. "Human conversation is the best thing for a baby."

"Aye," Jim said, "teaches 'em the best and the worst, but puts 'em to sleep every time!"

There was laughter.

"I've got a question," Bert said seriously. He looked at Ursula. "You mind if I ask you a question about all this? I've been wanting to for a while. I think we know each other well enough now."

Ursula folded her hands on her lap—Elaine knew this anxiety signal of hers—but her face remained placid, receptive.

"I was a pilot with the Air Force. American, of course. Got shot down early, got moved around from camp to camp, mostly between Sagan, Nuremburg, and Moosburg. Most Germans I knew were the bad kind, I'm sorry to say. I've always wondered what it was like for a regular German girl like yourself, just living day to day. I hope you don't mind me asking. You might not want to talk about it." What a strange kind of politeness Americans had—more a dare than kindness.

Elaine heard Salim in her inner ear. "Germans are just colonialists who lost power for a while." At the camp, he said he was tired of people talking about "the old holocaust," as he called it, when the *real* one was right here, right now.

Ursula leaned forward in her chair, crossing her slim legs the other way. "Yes, Germany had many faces during that time. I'm afraid I'm not a good source of information, however. I was a small child. All events were a big adventure that ended badly. I heard rumors of atrocities in death camps, but I was under the impression the Reich was forced into them by its enemies. My father was killed on the front, which made him a hero for a little while, but then Berlin was bombed, and we lost our flat. Life became very hard for us. We began to forget him, and we struggled to survive. I'm not sure this fully answers your question."

"No, it's just fine, thanks," the American said. "Just curious." Ursula still showed no emotion, although her very short answer implied discomfort. Bert had the class, at least, not to press her further.

There was a silence. Everyone sat for a moment, in front of the fire, contemplating the flickering light.

"Heroes! What a word." Ivy always spoke suddenly. "*Heroes* is a word for the men to sport about if they want it. Let a woman put the finishing touch on a man, but he doesn't have to be our God-blessed hero. The time he ran around sporting his armor and his weapons for the womenfolk better be long gone. Let him get in these nuclear wars, and do his terrorism, and throw his rocks for his own reasons. I won't have women being blamed in the end." Again, Elaine, only back for a few days after a year in Algiers, was shocked to think that maybe Ivy and Beatrice knew about Salim's leanings—that everyone had been talking about her husband when she wasn't in the room. Or was this, too, an overreaction on her part, like thinking Aunt Beatrice actually knew her plan for the château? Elaine had the sense that she didn't really know these people anymore, whether she'd known them for years, or just met them; she could not read them like she could read Benoît's weekend guests just a year or two ago. She had changed too much.

"Ivy, how do you manage to be old-fashioned and current at once?" Jim's husbandly chiding grin spread to Beatrice's face.

Ivy smiled and blew her nose. The sluicing sound reverberated in the room. Aunt Beatrice put her finger to her lips. Irina, with Ivy's sound, had stirred. All eyes went to her. There was a kind of collective sigh as the group saw that she was in deep sleep, her mouth open, her arms jutted out, fists clenched.

Aunt Beatrice leaned over and touched one of Irina's tiny hands. "Well, we're still good for something, aren't we?" she whispered to the baby. She touched Irina's hair and head gently. "She doesn't realize yet we're an old bunch of skeletons."

That's what they are, Elaine smiled inwardly—not mannequins, but skeletons. Salim would like that. In two weeks, he and she and the baby would go to America to raise money. Elaine couldn't wait for him to arrive here, then take her there. And yet . . . a warmth was in her as she felt the love of her child in this firelight. She didn't hate these people. They remembered a dead time, oblivious to the sufferings of the present—and yet there was comfort here. A kind of trance. Confusing, yes—Salim was right: this was a trance of complete denial of world reality.

Yet it gave little Irina a lullaby.

As if reading Elaine's mind—and giving Elaine goosebumps—Ivy said, "We sing a sweet song to the wee lass," leaning in, reaching out to touch a tiny leg, changing her voice to baby-talk. "Don't we, you pretty wee girl?"

Elaine's eyes met Ursula's. She could read nothing in the German woman's taut smile. Salim had said he liked her best of all of them.

Elaine pushed herself up off the couch. Her voice quiet, she thanked everyone for calming the baby. She murmured *bonne nuit* to all. Goodnights came back with kind smiles and again the little waves at the sleeping child. A silence followed Elaine and her baby through the room, through the tall wood door, out of the firelight and into the darkened dining room, then toward the stairway. As Elaine climbed the stairs, Aunt Beatrice called from behind her, "Elaine, *ma chère?*"

Elaine turned. Her aunt embraced her softly, so as not to wake Irina.

"I'm so glad you came," Aunt Beatrice said. "Your baby is so beautiful. So dark and different than we are, and that is good."

Blushing from the honesty and the sudden affection, Elaine thanked her. She yearned to ask, "Do you really know our plans?" but she just couldn't. It might ruin everything. Years ago,

Aunt Beatrice had been her great confidant; but no more, and especially not on the matter of the inheritance.

Aunt Beatrice looked about as if to say something, opening her mouth just slightly. Then she began to turn away.

But then she said, "I guessed your plans accurately, didn't I?"

"Plans about what?" Elaine temporized, lowering her voice to a whisper, as if the walls, should they hear, would exact revenge on her themselves.

"About razing this place."

Elaine looked into her aunt's eyes. 'Lie to her!' Salim would say. 'Don't risk the inheritance!'

Ingenuous words were about to come out, but then Elaine heard herself say: "I'm sorry, Beatrice. I . . . I don't know how I would keep the place when you're gone."

Surprising her niece, Aunt Beatrice embraced her gently again. "My dear, this place is absolutely impossible to keep up. I am too attached to do the right thing, but you, fortunately, you are a modern woman. You can let go of it."

"You're not angry?" Elaine found herself, completely without conscious thought, reaching her free hand to touch back a stray strand of her aunt's hair at the temple.

"I'm not angry, dear. From the grave, I will grieve. But no, I am not angry."

Should I tell her what we will do with the money? Elaine wondered. No. Elaine knew she couldn't say anything about that. Salim was no terrorist—he was an activist—but would Beatrice understand the difference? Would she understand that if you wanted to buy affordable housing for a thousand people who had been brought up in a camp, you would probably be helping some terrorists, young men who would then go on to hurt and kill? But how could you not help all the others too— all the women, children, and other men, family men, who were desperate to live the lives of human beings? Could Beatrice understand that the land had to be sold, condominiums established, joint ventures created, so that there was not only the initial money, but then continuing money to keep helping these desperate people of the colonized world? She would not understand—or maybe she would. But it was not necessary to try to make her. It was enough that Aunt Beatrice understood that Château Benoît would disappear.

"Beatrice," Elaine said heartfully. "You are brave. Brave to let go like this. I want to be like you." Elaine's eyes teared up; she saw similar tears in her aunt's eyes, and for the first time in the last forty-eight hours, she did not feel a disdainful distance from life here. She felt her old love of her aunt, and a deep freedom in her own soul.

"You are so beautiful, my dear," Beatrice whispered. She reached her hand to her niece's cheek and Elaine closed her eyes against the soft touch.

It seemed to Elaine that time stood still. A few moments before, leaving the old people behind, Elaine had wondered, with a confusion of regret and pleasure, how it had happened, yet again, that she herself had entered the dopey trance she'd always noticed when, as a child and adolescent, she had sat and watched young mothers sit restlessly with the old people. Now, as she felt the electricity of her aunt's affection—and more than that—her aunt's respect for her life's course, Elaine thought she had received a great gift, the gift of adulthood.

She opened her eyes and said to Aunt Beatrice, "I will always love you." Now Beatrice did cry, and so did Elaine. Irina slept through the tears.

"What will I do when you are gone?" Elaine said, then apologized. "I'm sorry."

"No, no, I understand."

"I will be alone," Elaine said.

"You will not be," Aunt Beatrice smiled, cupping Irina's head in her palm. "You will have this little girl."

"And my husband," Elaine said.

"Yes," Aunt Beatrice said graciously.

Elaine knew herself again suddenly, as she had before: a mother, a woman, and then a wife.

"I'll see you for breakfast," Aunt Beatrice smiled, returning to practical matters.

Elaine nodded. "See you then."

Aunt Beatrice gave Irina a kiss, kissed Elaine on both cheeks, and then turned back toward her guests.

Elaine, as if freed from a terrible cage of secrecy she did not even know she'd been in, glided up the stairs. She cradled Irina, turned her doorknob, and opened her door. She put Irina in the beautiful bassinet, handmade by Bert out of a fallen cottonwood from the east edge of the property, quilts and blankets made by Aunt Beatrice. Elaine sat there, gazing at a picture of her husband, whose smile was forced, as his smiles always were, his mind always on something serious. She felt released by her aunt, released to love her husband, released to adore her child. The utter wholeness of the feeling washed through her, sending a surge into her body; she wanted to yell out.

Elaine sat there a long time in the feeling, floating. She sang to Irina one of the songs her aunt had sung to her when she was young. And as she sang, she sang for herself for the future, and for the end to all secrets. She undressed, washed up, then turned off the lamp and climbed into bed. Falling asleep, she reminded herself that she'd be awake again in a few hours for feeding and changing. Drifting into sleep, she almost thought she heard her baby's cries.

But Elaine did not wake up again until eight hours later.

Irina Beatrice Zanoun, three months old, the most restless of sleepers until now, slept the whole night through, for the first time in her life.

the reincarnation
of donaldo fuertes

"Donald, you've got to be kidding!" laughed Ahmed Al-Azzazi (known as Gilbert Nakashi Washington until about six months ago), his colorful Muslim cap tight on his head, his blue jeans baggy almost to the knees, his shirt a blood-red, blood-orange mix of African colors. "Go to Spain? Tonight? The shape you're in? You're mad!"

The huge African-Asian-American youth and the tiny, wiry, old Spanish-American sat in Donald's study with their voices low so Fiora, Donald's wife, wouldn't hear. She and her women friends were socializing on the fire escape, as they did every Wednesday after church.

No doubt—and Donald knew it—he had gone a little mad since the accident, 'mad' in that old sense of the word, consumed by a passion or an idea. "I'm mad about going there, yes," Donald said. "But not like Captain Ahab—more like the Wright brothers."

He could see confusion on young Ahmed's wide black face, and in his strange, brownish-gray eyes.

Donaldo Fuertes was a librarian emeritus at New York Public Library's Fifth Avenue branch, the author of two books of poems, two books of translations, and a book of essays, *The Lion's Share*, for which he'd once been known in literary circles. Whereas he once wore dotted bow ties and black suspenders and pressed slacks, now his clothing had in it the vague wrinkle of someone aging and sick. He had never been impulsive. He still was not.

Except for this matter of getting to Spain.

"I've arranged everything." Donald pulled two airline tickets out of his book of Vallejo translations. "Fiora doesn't know."

Ahmed opened the airline ticket envelope: 4:43 a.m. departure to Barcelona. "Donald, you can't go anywhere these days without Darvon or your two canes. You really should have a wheelchair. How in the hell do you think you're going to—"

"I'm going to Barcelona, young man. Are you going with me?"

"Well, I mean, I *want* to, but I've got classes."

"We go for a week. I pay your expenses. You go back to school after that. *Huevos*, Ahmed. Find some balls!"

* * *

It was soon after their first meeting at the library that Donald saw a way to get to Spain through the boy. A month after Donald's small heart attack, Ahmed (still Gil then) asked for his autograph. Donald never learned much about the half African-American, half Vietnamese kid. Ahmed was not talkative about his past life except to say that he disliked his family. But to have an able-bodied young man along in Spain—a young man who had lived overseas most of his life (albeit in Asia), a young philosophy graduate student, who knew how to carry on a meaningful conversation—what could be better?

Donald recalled himself as Donaldo when he thought of Spain, young Donaldo whose impulses had caused those deaths long ago. He did not tell Ahmed why he wished to return to his old country after so long, or of his need to test, at the graves, the possibility of redemption; but these were never far from his own mind, an aging man who had not returned to his homeland for more than the length of time this young American had been alive.

The boy was always polite, and he spoke English not like a ghetto boy, but like the foreign service brat he was. Granted, he looked a little rebellious—cutting his smooth black hair short, save for a little ponytail braided down the nape of his neck; wearing an earring and T-shirts (nothing but T-shirts then before converting). He was very smart, with slightly slanting eyes, wire-rimmed glasses, his skin somehow black and brown at once.

"He's almost as bright as I am," Donald once quipped to Fiora. "Almost."

Ahmed was half American, but he meditated, and his intellect smelled of Zen and koans and gurus. This, of course, could not continue now that he had decided to be a Muslim. When Donald inquired after the transition, Ahmed said, "I'm trying to absorb my past into my new present, but the Zen is already disappearing from my life." Though Donald thought the boy would find other old men to listen to (and indeed, Ahmed talked of them more and more now—men he called his *mousyed*, spiritual teachers) he still came around to 17th Street in Chelsea to talk to, and be of service to, an old Spanish man. Donald gathered there were five sacred tasks Ahmed must perform. Somehow, Donald was one of these tasks, though even at his most cynical, he did think the boy loved him.

"Enjoy him," Fiora advised. "I know I do." Fiora had grown sick of hearing every graphic detail of the car wreck—Donald walking around the corner, the *swiiiissssh* of the skid, the limousine jumping the curb, Donald's flight through the window of Archibald & Fields, Architects, the contents of his briefcase strewn everywhere. Fiora had grown tired of walking with Donald back to the site of the accident; but the boy had endless patience.

"You all clean me," Donald would complain, "and wipe my ass and my balls and toss my feces out in pans and talk to me like a child. There is a kind of jaundice in my once-smooth Latin brown complexion"—Donald would point to his shriveling arms—"You see? I tell you, Ahmed, I was once a dandy! And now my head is full of straw. Who said that?"

"T. S. Eliot," the boy responded.

"Exactly. I will educate you in our European culture if it is the last thing I do. I tell my neighbors, '*Estoy entre dos aguas.*' They think I stand between the waters of illness and health. But I mean something else. You know this, Ahmed, eh? I stand between the waters of life and death, like every good poet."

"You do, Donald. You're really something. Allah has made you great."

A few nights later, Donald whispered to Fiora, "He seems to worship me. Though he worships Allah more. Oh well, neither worship will last. He'll find a new god in a few years. And he'll become sick of the smell of my rotting limbs and breath. Sick of the old man's complaints. Every relationship but yours and mine seems to end, Fiora."

* * *

Let's hope not tonight, Donald thought, fingering the tickets on the desk. Let's hope not for another week. Finally, thirty-eight years after leaving Spain, I have found the balls to go back, and I have this young, strong, deep-thinking man to help me. It is time to make my peace with my youthful errors.

"We'll go to your apartment for your things," Donald said. "Okay? Then we'll go to the airport. Fiora will think we've gone out for a walk. Stop worrying! You act worried, but I think you're flinching at the thought of some *real* responsibility. In dreams begin responsibilities! Let me tell you something, Ahmed." (Months after his Muslim transformation, Donald had finally become comfortable with the boy's new name.) "Five years ago, I delivered my granddaughter Elsepina on a family camping trip, delivered her directly out of my daughter's womb. No doctor anywhere. Fiora and Jimmy off for groceries. I pulled my own blood out of my own blood. Raphaela was very tired after we finished. She wiped the rank and bloody child and she said, 'Papa, you have magic fingers.' Do you see now what I'm saying?"

Ahmed pushed his glasses up his nose—his polite way of shrugging.

"Responsibilities! I who knew so little about the woman's body (though it never stopped me from writing about it), I took this sudden responsibility of birthing my grandchild, this sudden responsibility forced upon me, and I've never been the same. I grew up at age sixty. This is what I mean. *Huevos*, Ahmed."

The boy would come around. He had never been to Europe, only Asia. He was curious about the seat of the West. He would come around.

"Let me say this, Ahmed, then I'll let you be. You remember what your mother wrote to your aunt? You remember? It is indelible in my mind, this small fact I have managed to learn about you."

Ahmed frowned. "Not the letter. Don't bring that up again."

"I must. 'Who knows,' she wrote, 'what Gil's angry at these days? Moving around all the time? Being an only child? Being deprived of Western culture and American hamburgers? The fact that we threw out his father's Islam and my Buddhism, raising him an atheist? His father? Me? By the time he's ready to be gentle with me, he'll be forty, with children of his own, a man who has finally cut through his undergrowth. He'll want to forgive me, but I'll be gone.' Do you remember, Ahmed?"

"Of course, Donald." The boy always frowned at the mention of his family. "What are you saying?"

"I am talking about why you must come to Spain with me. My business. I am talking about family tragedy and forgiveness. I will show you something in Spain. I will take you to a place. I promise you"—Donald leaned toward him—"if you come to Spain with me, you will understand yourself better. I have thrown a Socratic gauntlet down. Take it up. I'll give you what you have been trying to get from everything . . . including from Islam."

"The truth? That Allah is great in all things? Spain will show me this? I know this already."

"Spain will show you truth, my young Mohammed."

The boy stared, frowning, into Donald's eyes. "You are really something. You really want me to go?"

"Donaldo?" Fiora called from the fire escape. "Ahmed? Is Donald alright in there, Ahmed?"

"Yes, Mrs. Fuertes," the boy called out the window. "We're just talking."

"Let's put him to bed soon."

"Okay, Mrs. Fuertes," Ahmed called out. He lowered his voice, "Just tell me this, Donald. What's so important in Spain anyway? I have so much else going on right now. I mean, I want to help you, I really do. But what's going on in Spain?"

Donald waggled his finger. "No, no. Think of it as an unfolding story. I will not tell you everything now. You come to Spain. I take you to a place. Your life is changed. That is what I can offer. Whether you go or not, mind you, I will go."

Ahmed reached back to twirl his ponytail. He ran his tongue around inside his mouth.

"You're really going to go, no matter what. Even if it kills you?" He picked up the tickets again, confirming for the umpteenth time that the Air Iberia flight left LaGuardia tonight, at 4:43 a.m.

Donald nodded with certainty. "I will go."

"I have to admit," Ahmed said, "a free trip to Spain . . . it sounds tempting. But why not tell Fiora?"

"She's too protective. She wouldn't let me go."

Donald sat back in his chair, watched Ahmed's mind at work behind the gray eyes. Donald crossed his arms over his chest and listened to the murmur of voices from the balcony as the boy closed his eyes to consider his final decision.

"Yes," Ahmed said finally, "I'll do it. But you take a little nap first, and we turn back if you have the slightest problem. And you leave Fiora a note. If you don't want me to tell her, I won't. But you have to leave her some kind of note."

"Well, alright," Donald lamented. He would leave a note that they were going for a walk before bedtime. The boy wouldn't know the difference.

II

Now the street lay dark and quiet in the balmy night breeze. Donald walked slowly with two canes beside the tall, broad Ahmed Al-Azzazi. The sound of Manhattan, like the whirring rumble of a generator, got louder as they reached 6th Avenue, louder still as a subway rumbled under them. Donald moved with cramped, pained movements, like a crippled spider. A huge neon clock up the avenue read eleven-thirty p.m.

A northbound subway waited downstairs with its doors open. Donald dropped into a seat next to a well-dressed black man reading the *Daily News*. Donald closed his eyes, listening to the subway rumble and screech below. The painkillers he had taken earlier gave him a slight tipsiness and relaxed his aching leg and arm muscles.

"How do you feel?" Ahmed whispered.

"Fine. But I'll rest in the park. You go up to your place and get your things. I'll avoid your stairs." Donald had packed nothing, so as not to arouse Fiora's suspicion—only shoved a book in each jacket pocket (his Vallejo translations for sentiment and a Len Deighton thriller for airplane reading). He would buy necessities in Spain. The boy, on the other hand, had ample time to get some clothes and toiletries. Why spend money on the boy, who lived with his aunt just near the park? Let Ahmed fill a daypack with his things on the way to the airport. This had been the plan, and they would stick with it, but Donald realized now he did not want to go up to the apartment. He just wanted to sit a minute in the clear, night air. And he suspected that Ahmed had missed either the evening or the night prayer—Donaldo got them mixed up, though he remembered that one was called *maghrib* and the other *isha*. Let the boy go up to his room and get his ablutions out of the way.

"My building has an elevator," Ahmed offered, though he knew Donald would refuse. "The park's dangerous at night, Donald."

"You know how I despise elevators. I'll sit in the park. There are benches just in from the Plaza Hotel, very well lit. Don't worry. I'll be in no danger there."

People exaggerated the dangers of Central Park. They had done so for thirty years. Besides, his money and the tickets were safely hidden in a money belt under his shirt.

As they came up the subway steps, Donald panting from the short climb, cabs and limos turned corners and stopped in front of the Plaza. Two hansoms sat together at the entrance to the park across the street, the drivers smoking and talking atop the carriages. Donald steeled himself for the walk across the street, refusing Ahmed's help. Progressing across the crosswalk, he yelled at a honking car, its driver protesting the slow waddle of an old man. Stepping onto the parkside curb, Donald felt a breeze chill his sweaty face, wrists, and under his socks.

Some transients slept on benches along the wooded walkway into the park. Donald sat down on a slightly damp bench. After Ahmed left at a jog for his place on 59th, Donald took stock from his seat. The tramp on the bench to the left was snoring. On the bench across from him, seated in a lotus position, was a young man, Caucasian, blond-haired, meditating—arms equally bowed at each side, connecting with knees, thumb, and middle fingers in circles. Months ago, this would have been Gil the Buddhist. Donald had tried meditation over the years, preferring prayer. Meditation, if not denying, at least eschewed the presence of a personal, kind, revengeful, cunning God. If there were no God whom humanity resembled, life made little sense.

Donald pulled the paperback of Vallejo translations out of his jacket pocket. It had sold well, published just as Latin American writing began its invasion into American letters. Donald couldn't read the book in the dim light but found with his fingers the dog-ear at the poem "Our Daily Bread," one of Vallejo's most difficult to translate. The Darvon was making him drowsy, and he dropped his head to his chest, picturing himself in a couple days, standing on the Costa Brava, on the ridge just north of Barcelona. Donald saw himself standing in the ocean breeze, the Vallejo book open, reading to Ahmed the sentimental lines:

> "In this cold hour, when the earth
> transcends human dust, so sorrowful,
> I want to beat on all the doors
> and beg pardon from someone,
> and make fresh bread with it
> in the oven of my heart . . ."

The old man would murmur to the sea, tell his story and weep. The Muslim boy, a little distant, unsure but caring, would comfort him.

Donald put down the book and leaned his head back to find the edge of the bench, letting the Darvon and exhaustion run through him.

"Got it, man."

Half asleep, Donald heard the voice at a distance. Not Ahmed's voice. Someone with a Hispanic accent. The fingers of God reached into his jacket pocket. Donald opened his eyes, grabbing the wrist with a feeble hand.

"*Puta cabrón!*" The teenager smacked Donald across the forehead with the wallet he had just taken from the old sleeping man's breast pocket.

Pain shot down into Donald's neck, and he hunched over. "*Dios!*" Donald cried. "Stop that!" He grabbed his head. *Could this be happening?* There were two of them, their shirts cut above the navels, one Latino, one black.

"Let's book!" the second teenager said.

The boys grabbed Donald's canes, and in seconds were gone.

Donald's eyes filmed over with pain, and he reached for the Darvon. At least they hadn't had time to take that out of his other breast pocket. Holding his wounded head—feeling the bump and a trace of liquid there—Donald tried to remember how many Darvon he had taken in the last hour. This would make four. He had five hundred dollars in travelers checks in his money belt and his American Express card there. But the Visa and Mastercard were gone in the wallet, and two hundred dollars cash, and the canes.

Donald tried to stand. How could he walk without the canes? So suddenly, a man goes from Joshua to Job. "Gil," he whispered, leaning against some shrubs for breath. He fell against a tree.

Cars rushed around beyond the shrubbery. Someone whistled for a cab. The squeal of tires, a door slamming. Donald tried to move, tried to catch his breath.

"Donald? What happened?" Ahmed ran over from the park entrance, pushing a daypack up his arm.

"Hooligans," Donald panted. "They took my canes, my wallet. What was I thinking! It should not have happened— tonight!" Pain numbed his head and left shoulder, and his lower-back brace dug into the skin of his sides and stomach. The boy kneeled down next to him.

"This is real bad," Ahmed cried. "I *knew* something would happen. Allah, bring healing. I bear witness that there is no God but Allah. I bear witness that Mohammed is the Messenger of God. I ask for healing."

Donald told himself to breathe deeply, to let the Darvon work. Ahmed was blotting his head wound with a handkerchief.

"I *knew* it!" Ahmed hissed. "Real responsible of me, leaving you here."

Donald reached into the side pocket of his jacket. He was taking too many Darvon. He wouldn't be able to get on the plane if he was unconscious.

"We must get to a phone," Donald said. "I must call the credit-card companies."

"Okay," Ahmed nodded vigorously. "I'll take you back to your place."

"No! Not home! To *your* apartment. We will use your phone. We will rest. We will take a cab to the airport, not the subway. This adventure has begun badly, but it will not end."

"Donald, we have to go to *your* house. You've got no canes. You're crazy to push yourself like this."

"No!" Donald hissed. "We will continue my . . . pilgrimage . . . my Haj." His ears rung, and he reached his hand up and felt a bump where the corner of the wallet had hit him. "We'll go to your flat in a cab."

Ahmed lifted him, half-dragging him toward the park entrance. "We have to call the police."

"They'll find nothing, and we won't make the plane. Get a cab."

As Ahmed hailed a cab, Donald warned, "Don't tell the driver how far we're going. He won't take us three blocks."

The pain of bending into the cab was like a cloak of fire. Donald let his head fall back against the seat. "Go around the park once," he whispered. Maybe they would see the teenagers. And it would drive up the cab fare.

The cab smelled vaguely of rancid food, the cabbie's head visible over the seat, bald with wisps of hair at the rim and down to the neck. The black, plastic ends of his glasses glinted behind his ears.

The cab ride gave Donald some relief, and he felt his head clearing slightly. There was no turning back. It was 12:26. When they got to Ahmed's apartment, he could rest a little, then get to the airport and onto the plane where he could sleep for hours.

At Donald's signal, Ahmed instructed the driver to return to 59th. But Ahmed seemed uncertain, as if he wanted to steer them back to Fiora. Was the boy tempted to betray the mission? Was young Mohammed going to become a betrayer?

"Come, Ahmed," Donald managed, "you were speaking earlier about Frobenius. What do you see in Frobenius' theory?"

Ahmed laughed. "You want to talk philosophy now?"

"Of course," Donald said, gripping Ahmed's wrist as he pulled himself up in the seat. "Distract me with some philosophy."

It was a smart move. The boy grinned. "You are one strong *hombre*."

"Strong for an old man. Frobenius. Tell me what you are writing in your research."

Ahmed took a deep breath. About himself, he wouldn't talk. But about philosophy—especially his long research essay for his Western philosophy class—he always talked.

"Well, you know," he began, "during your lifetime, especially beginning when you were a boy, Spengler and *The Waste Land* and the dark side of existentialism, the dark unconscious of Freud, World War I, all the monarchies and old social systems were dissolving, and rational culture seemed to be disintegrating, then Stalin kills twenty million, and the Holocaust comes. But in the midst of all this, there's Frobenius. Frobenius, this prophet of hope . . ."

Nothing more beautiful, Donald thought, than a young mind rising out of the rock, half-sculpted, dusted in the patina of white and gray, its tongue licking the past off its lips; all the more beautiful because the old minds must have gone, already, through their refining fires.

". . . the final stage of old culture . . . then an ontology of reconstruction . . . but the thing is, is all this possible, or is it just hopefulness without reason . . ."

Donald nodded, watching the city pass around him, not really listening, snugly enclosed for a second in the glass case of the cab windows. As the cab's front wheel, shooting the car upward, scraped the curb on 59th, he had begun to doze off. He opened his eyes, fighting the heaviness of his lids. If he fell asleep, Ahmed would make that reason enough to take him home.

Ahmed stopped his words in the middle of a thought, paid the cabbie, and helped Donald out.

"You sure he's alright?" the cabbie asked. "Looks like you oughta take him to a hospital."

"I'm alright," Donald said, "I'm allowed an adventure, aren't I? Now leave us alone."

III

They stood in front of a fancy restaurant, a basement place with a doorman at the top of its steps. Ahmed pointed up to the building across the street. "My aunt's place is there." The building was elegant, with a deep green tarpaulin vestibule, calligraphed number, a very tall doorman.

Donald knew it had six flights of stairs. He had been claustrophobic most of his life; elevators were more frightening, especially tonight, than he could handle. He would have to walk up the steps. To Ahmed he said, "You'll help me up the stairs. No elevator."

"Of course."

First, Ahmed helped him across the busy street. Donald had the vague sense of himself as flowing out and away from things, a ship leaving the shore, a lover waving to him from the receding beach. He feared the feeling. Focusing on the tall, dark-haired doorman who saw their approach, Donald said, "He was taller than the others were . . ." Donald cleared his throat of phlegm. "What poet is that?"

Ahmed grinned. "Wait. That's a hard one. Shit, I know that one."

"You don't know," Donald challenged. "Here is a hint. I translated the poem. It is a name from another country."

Ahmed grinned triumphantly. "It's the Swedish guy, right? Swedenborg. Borges' poem called 'Swedenborg.'"

"Very good." Donald smiled. "As long as you can correctly identify my test quotes, student Ahmed Al-Azzazi, you will keep an old man alive. As soon as you fail, I die. How does that sound for drama?" Stepping up to the curb, a car whizzing past, Donald looked at his watch. There was definitely still time. He would rest upstairs. And there was the call to the credit-card companies.

"Donald," Ahmed said, frowning, "that's a weird thing to say."

"Oh, come now. Just a joke. Old men at death's door make such jokes. I should get some rest now, Ahmed. We'll go to your place. I will lie out on the couch for a brief time. And we must make a call."

"We'll be alright," Ahmed told the doorman, who was indeed quite tall, and responded with a "Good morning" in a thick Eastern European or Russian accent, opening the glass door.

Neither Ahmed nor Donald spoke as they laboriously ascended the first flight of stairs. At the top of the second, Ahmed offered to do what, a few months ago, he had done many times. Exhausted and woozy, Donald let the boy pick him up and carry him in strong arms.

Ahmed lay him on a couch in a dim living room, street noises slightly distant outside the open window. Ahmed asked if he could read aloud to him from the essay he'd been working on. Donald tried to listen but couldn't. He heard bits, "the eye and the heart," "sin and allegory," "the Muslim view of suffering," but couldn't enjoy the intensity. The boy must have realized it because he put the papers down and quietly rocked in his rocking chair, which creaked with each undulation. The digital VCR clock read 12:59.

Donald woke up to the sound of a loud, bass-vibrating car radio passing outside. A thick purple afghan lay over him and the VCR read 1:50. Ahmed had gone, leaving a note on top of a manuscript that carried the byline Ahmed Al-Azzazi and the phrase "Written in praise of Allah the most holy."

The note was written in a careful hand: "I'm going to get some replacement canes for you down on Bleecker Street. Here's the manuscript I've been telling you about."

Donald felt under his brace for the money belt and the envelope of plane tickets. Everything was still there. He closed his eyes, images coming of his father's tiny office near the east station, then of a journey by ship, Vallejo with the loyalists in the north, Fiora in a grocery store, the limousine jumping over the curb at him, a car flying off a Costa Brava cliff decades ago . . . images coming and fading and coming again.

Perhaps sleeping any more is a mistake, he thought suddenly. Perhaps I won't wake up on time. He opened his eyes, pushed himself up. In the bathroom, he splashed water on his face, again and again, murmuring to himself to stay awake. He rubbed the cut on his forehead with wet toilet paper until the pain helped him awaken.

By now Fiora would be sleeping deeply, accustomed to his long night walks. She would feel betrayed in the morning when she found the note in the study. But she would understand. And he would call her as soon as they landed in Barcelona. Why had he resisted going with her instead of this young man? She was such a worrier. He loved her, but this was better.

Donald returned to the couch. The living room was peach-colored, Native American crafts on end tables, wicker chairs, a huge trapezoid-shaped coffee table, brown leather easy chairs, an antique china cabinet, Native American rugs and wall hangings, and framed posters with various names of exhibitions and paintings. It was Gil's aunt's taste he saw here, not Ahmed's. On the coffee table lay a picture book about Taos, New Mexico—

next to it, a small glass-framed picture of a woman, presumably the aunt, leaning against a Spanish-style building. Ahmed had once said his aunt lived half the year in New Mexico. She was there now. Ahmed seemed to respect her taste in her absence, letting it be as she left it, though on the coffee table there was a large, embossed Quran, and on a shelf there was a large picture of a bearded Muslim man—Ahmed's *mullah*? His Imam? What were all the different names and titles these Muslim teachers had? Donald could never remember.

Donald turned on a lamp and lifted the boy's papers. His headache had receded somewhat. The manuscript was thick, some 150 pages. I want to keep my mind active, Donald thought with a smile, but this is a little much. Ah well, at least it will keep me awake. Donald opened the pages at random, to 76. These pages were the first piece of original work Ahmed had ever shown him. Would they be brilliant?

IV

"To be alone, what is that? To be alone so long you invite anything in that will prosper? That is what Western 'modernity' had been, child of broken centuries, child of alienation, absorbing new experience like a sponge, saturated to the point of leaking, a flood of consciousness. And now we sit at the brink of post-modernism. Yet what is that? Isn't it more of the same materialistic rapture and avoidance of Allah?

"Donaldo Fuertes, a modern who once tried to rise to heights, to be more than modern, wrote in *The Lion's Share*, 1986: 'If we are to have vision as we enter the twenty-first century, it must be of the hermit returning to his community, after a century of exile.'

"Unfortunately, Mr. Fuertes' *The Lion's Share* stops short of providing a matrix for repatriation—one wishes the quoted sentence had been in Fuertes' introduction rather than conclusion. The age of alienation, the modern age, which began with Nietzsche's *Beyond Good and Evil* in 1886, must end. We must enter a new age, but not the quiet New Age we have now. We must enter an age of pure understanding, as outlined in the Quran.

"Some thinkers of my generation ask: How shall we reconstruct Western mythology as a century of broken mythologies drags us into self-destruction? These thinkers turn to Joseph Campbell and his disciples and are satisfied to gather myths and preach mythic world unity. Jungians, they still and always believe there are myths somewhere to live by.

"I say, postmodernism must do more; must finally prove to Western culture (what modernism set out but failed to do) that the myths by which we have lived are illusion; must retrace our history from Ancient beyond Modern, to postmodern, to de-mystification. As we enter the twenty-first century of cyberpunk and digital music, the heroes of modernism, the lovers of myth, the Donaldo Fuerteses must die out. To be postmodern is to be mythless, not to distrust everything—that's just juvenile rebellion—but to distrust all *mythos*, to believe only in the revealed Truth. In the search for truth, when I look into the lion's mouth, I must be naked of illusion, so the lion, rising from its sleep, will not take me by my string of cloth. This Fuertes and the moderns did not do. The lion of illusion took them. To attain demystification, I must suffer, both as the predator and the prey. To be the beaten Jew is not enough. Only as I regret the exhilaration I felt beating the Jew, will I know pleasure.

"In the face of a call to arms, the Western modernist will ask: Are our white, Anglo, colonialist ancestors and inheritance falling against us so hard without embrace, that we cannot combine the freedom of our huge present with the authority of the past? Must we build the holy city by destroying the town? Is there not something to retain in old Western myths as we smother them with the Truth of Islam, which rises above all West and all East?

"My answer is: Plan the end. We must destroy everything Western and everything Eastern. We've gone wrong and we must clean the slate. We will not have any new paradigm without some disaster. We must raze the town if we want a new city. Thinkers of my generation must not be afraid of their loneliness. They must celebrate it. It is surrender to Allah."

Donald lifted his eyes, surprised by the click of the VCR underneath the television. The crazy boy must have set it to record something before he left. At three o'clock in the morning?

Donald read further on in the manuscript. My God, he sighed, what abstract, silly shit! How had this seemingly intelligent boy produced such claptrap? Was Gil Washington, a.k.a. Ahmed Al-Azzazi, like all the other young people these days, a child of television, a child of imagination, not intelligence? And what power this Islam must have on him.

Donald closed his eyes. He laughed, too shocked to do anything else. He had thought the boy a concrete thinker, an intelligent philosopher. What happened to the intelligence of Frobenius? I was jealous of *this* boy? What a night. Going to Spain, getting mugged, the boy demystified! Donald opened his eyes, shaking his head in wonder. Impulsiveness upset the routine of reality and caused these wrinkles, and everything changed.

What would he say to Ahmed? The boy would certainly ask if his elderly mentor had read these papers. Donald couldn't be too critical. He couldn't say, "Thank you for spitting in the face of the modern vision I have worked all my life toward." My God,

Donald thought suddenly, can I go to Spain with this boy? But, now, what choice did he have? The boat had left the shore, as the saying went.

"It will be a good challenge for you, Donald," he murmured to himself, leafing randomly to page 97, ". . . the eye and heart, which are enemies, make aesthetics unnecessary . . ."

"You must treat it as nothing special," he murmured to himself, "a senseless rebellion. Don't take this personally."

He heard footsteps outside the door, the scraping of the key. Put on a face to meet the face, he thought, putting the papers down and pushing himself up.

"Hey, Donald. You're up." The boy smiled, holding two canes in one hand and a bag in another. "I got some things. Did the machine go on?" He looked under the television, confirming it. "An Imam from the Saudi-based mosque is preaching tonight on the Islamic Broadcasting Network."

"You are recording him?" Donald asked, hoping to move conversation away from the manuscript.

"Yeah. Did you sleep alright? Don't you want to sit down?" Ahmed handed the canes over. They were shiny black with no ornamentation. "I got them at an all-night S & M place on Bleecker Street," he said disgustedly. "The Bondage Banquet. No hardware stores were open that I could find. What a sick culture we live in." He walked into the kitchen with the paper bag.

Moving toward a small kitchen, separated from the living room by a counter and high stools, Donald sat on a stool. Ahmed had bought wine, cottage cheese, and bread.

"May I have a bowl of the cottage cheese?" Donald asked.

"Of course." The boy tore the plastic rim off the perimeter of the lid. He scooped the cheese into a bowl and found a spoon. "I always put raisins in mine," Ahmed said. "You want some?"

"That would be nice," Donald nodded.

Donald noticed again—but after the essay it made a little more sense—raw red skin on the boy's brown fingernails from biting them. Donald regretted, suddenly, that Ahmed was always so silent, such a good listener, only talking obliquely about his own life and past. Donald had not pried. But what would make a boy wish for the decimation of all that was?

Ahmed handed Donald the bowl of cottage cheese and moved out of the kitchen to the living room. "How are you feeling?"

Slowly, Donald swiveled his stool. "I'm feeling quite well. The rest did me good. I'll make it to the plane."

"How's your head?"

"It hurts, but I'll be alright."

There was silence. Ahmed picked up the pages of his essay. "Did you read some of this? What did you think?"

Now the challenge, Donald thought. He quipped, "'You are pulling the covers up over my head, you are trying to bury me! Who was that?"

"That's easy," Ahmed said with a frown. "Kafka, 'The Judgment.' I suppose you could feel that way. But I don't want to bury the past—I want to explode it! I am called to find a new vision. You know? Islam gives me that."

Donald nodded. The manuscript was so raw, a young man's wound. Any criticism at all would rankle. But a little rankling couldn't hurt. "It is ironic, isn't it? You're helping me do this crazy dangerous thing, going off to Spain, when it can do nothing but debilitate me and move me closer to dying. The same thing your essay tries to do."

"Donald, you're not going to die. You'll make it to Spain. Have you called your credit-card company?"

"I did before I slept. I'm alright. This essay . . ." Leave it alone, Fiora would tell him, you'll ruin things. "When did you begin writing it?"

"About a month and a half ago. I've been writing it off and on since. I wrote about thirty pages last summer, of another essay—nothing this powerful. Then I got the Western philosophy assignment about six weeks ago."

"You and I met last summer," Donald thought aloud.

"I met you in July, just after I read *The Lion's Share*. I started writing the other essay after I read *Lion*. I guess you inspired me to think deeply about things. But there wasn't truth in that first essay. I realized that when I discovered Allah. I threw it away and began this one."

So many sarcasms flew into Donald's mind that he had to bite his lip to stop them. "Well, I think this is an interesting beginning to something," he offered. "Shall we continue our discussion on the way to the airport?" He pointed to the VCR clock: 3:16.

"I guess you're really going to Spain, huh?" Ahmed stacked the papers. "I can't really believe it."

"Why not? We won't let a little exhaustion stop us. I have *life* left in me!"

Ahmed laughed. "You're great, Donald. I mean, I thought you'd be offended by the essay."

"Surprised," Donald said, "but not offended. Perhaps gurus should get to know their students better. Or should I say, *Sayahouds* should."

One week, Donald thought. Just last one week with this boy. *Of course, I'm offended.* Almost, for a moment, he felt his passion for Spain dissipate. It was more than physical exhaustion. Almost, for a moment, he wanted to run back to 17th Street.

"I'll call a cab," Ahmed said, picking up the phone.

A few minutes later, they waddled down the stairs—Donald refusing to be carried, though he had needed help getting his jacket on—and stood on the sidewalk, waiting for the cab, a cool breeze touching their sweat. Donald shuddered as he bent into the cab, laying his new canes across his lap.

"We are almost in Barcelona," Donald said. "What else can happen?"

"Nothing," the boy agreed. "LaGuardia," he instructed the cab driver, asking Donald for the tickets.

The cabbie, Donald noticed, wore a Muslim cap, and seemed, from his ID, to be from Libya.

V

They arrived at the airport at 3:50. It was uncrowded but nonetheless very bright. Donald sat down in a black leather lobby chair with the boy's pack on his lap, while Ahmed stood in the relatively short "No Luggage" line for check in. Donald was thankful that his passport had been in his money belt. The clerk had required him to show it at the counter, making him rise, walk there, walk back. It was not enough for Ahmed to point to him.

In a few minutes, Ahmed returned, saying, "I ordered you a wheelchair."

Donald put on a show of refusal but gave in. He had begun to feel morose and fighting that off took more energy than anything. He had wanted to go to Spain with an ally, not a strange enemy. God is punishing you, Donald thought to himself. Allah is laughing. You manipulated this boy into helping you, and now you have been avenged!

At the Iberian Air gate, there was a crowd of bleary-eyed travelers. Nearly all the chatter—between a mother and her children, two businessmen, and two women who had just met each other—was in different accents of Spanish.

Ahmed, for some reason, had become restless, looking back toward the security gates and on past, as if looking for something. Ahmed had been searched by the security people there.

"Have you lost something?" Donald asked.

"No, no," Ahmed said. "Just can't believe we're actually here. You know, after the last few hours, even I'm exhausted. You must be really tired."

"Yes," Donald said, "but that's alright. I'm having my last death surge." He grinned, waiting for the boy to reprimand his moribund humor.

"Donald," Ahmed asked, "will you tell me why you're going to Spain?"

Strange, Donald thought. The boy didn't usually ask direct questions. And again, the boy stole an irritating glance behind. "I know I'm being impatient. But I'm really curious. It must be something really big."

"Ah yes, it's something for Geraldo Rivera." Telling the boy would end the suspense just a bit early. But might not telling him also close some of the strange distance that had arisen since the essay? "What a night it's been, eh?"

"Oh yes." The boy had a pleasant laugh. One would never have known he had become something of a fanatic.

Donald closed his eyes, clasping his hands on his stomach. Tell the boy, try to remember when you were young. Didn't you, at times, write things that ended up having nothing, really, to do with what you ultimately believed? Weren't you actually crying out for someone older and wiser to rise above your excrement and have faith in you?

"I will tell you something, Ahmed. You know why I came to America, yes?"

"I know a little. Your parents died in a car accident when you were sixteen. You always wanted to study in America."

"Generally, yes. You might say those are enough motivation for making the journey. But why do you think I've never gone back to Spain?"

"I don't know."

"Ah, well. Here it is, then. I came to America to be reincarnated. I had caused three deaths, and I had survived three deaths, but I had come away without my . . . let's say, without my soul. That will sound melodramatic to you. Or perhaps, I think now, it will not.

"My brother, my parents, and I were driving on vacation on the Spanish coast. I was nearly a young man, sixteen years old. But like a stupid child, I leaned forward, to point at a passing Russian freighter, and my arm crossed my father's field of vision. I remember it quite vividly. I still feel . . ." Donald rubbed his left elbow ". . . the touch of my father's nose on my bare arm. I startled him, knocked him back accidently. The car swerved, running off the road, over the cliff. I was thrown clear, but the others were not. I caused three deaths that day.

"Fifty years later, I was in a second car accident. That second accident showed me that the first was not yet put to bed. All my life I had fled it, but then at sixty-five, that accident on 17th Street—I believe I sought it out, this pain to myself, as a punishment. This is the utter complexity of the human soul."

Ahmed was shaking his head. "You mean that you unconsciously, purposely, got hit by the limousine? You're saying something very serious, Donald."

"Is it not possible? If you do not forgive yourself for something you have done in the past, don't you perhaps invite it again? First you rebel and rant and rave, then you calm down, as all young people do when they reach middle age. Ah, but the wounds are not gone. My life has always been stained with a sense of guilt from that summer afternoon. This is why I have always loved Vallejo's poetry. He knows guilt. In 'Black Messengers' he writes:

> *We turn our eyes as if*
> *summoned by a tap on the shoulder;*
> *we turn mad eyes and all experience*
> *wells up like a pool of guilt in our gaze.*

"Vallejo knew how, even if we have *not* done something as terrible as I did, all of us seek to rectify guilt. Somehow, we are God's creatures but do not believe we deserve life. You see what I mean?"

Ahmed nodded at the possibility.

"What do we need in order to rectify that guilt? If we are thinking people, we need honesty. Augustine has these lines, in 'Late Have I Loved Thee': 'Thou wert within and I was without. I was looking for Thee out there, and I threw myself, deformed as I was, upon those well-formed things which Thou made. But I did not find you.' Coming over from Spain at seventeen, I remember *un mar alborotado*, a rough sea journey. I thought I would throw myself on America and find a new life there. Once here in America, I did everything American, wore American clothes, loved America. I even wrote in English, which was the biggest mistake. English is the preferred language of my tongue, but not my soul.

"Later, in my middle age, I found I had settled in a Spanish building—as if by instinct I'd been moving *back* into the self I had lost in those first years of throwing myself onto America's land of well-formed things. But I never could find my way back to my soul. I never quite made peace with myself, I never quite forgave myself, never quite healed my history, as I think you have not done."

Donald looked into Ahmed's eyes. Ahmed, mastered for a moment, looked down.

"I have never been a happy man, Ahmed, never felt whole. I will wager you have lost a little of your soul too, through family pain and tragedy. Like everyone else, you have a history that needs healing, a dark history that makes you bite your nails, kowtow to an old man's whims, dive into Islam.

"So, you see—all this is why I want you to go with me to Spain. So you can see and grow and not make the mistakes I made. You will find your place, your renewal, deep in here, listening to the *silent* voice of your heart." Donald was startled by the poking strength of his finger in his own bony solar plexus.

Ahmed looked behind again with jerking eyes. "Why does it always come down to that 'still silent voice within?' Popular mysticism. It's really hokey."

"But true."

"No." Ahmed's face was screwed up as if he'd come upon a bad smell. "I mean, you're projecting your own unhappiness onto me, right? Then you come up with the Alan Watts, Ram Dass 'listen to the still silent voice within.' Old people always do that. I'm a happy person. Islam is my happiness."

"I haven't meant to offend you." Donald sighed.

"You haven't offended me. It just sounds like you're into Joseph Campbell's 'find your bliss,' that sort of thing. Being like that's not the key to life. A man should be torn between life's forces, a man should try to become a force as powerful as the worst the universe can throw against him. If I can withstand anything the universe and Allah are capable of, then I'm real. I want to be real. Your still silent voice is like Cheerios and McDonald's and Diet Coke. I'm in revolt."

Donald was exhausted, down to his bones. Let's just get to Spain, he wanted to say. No conversation, no expectations, just you help me walk to some graves. Somehow, we'll salvage this adventure.

"You know Donald . . ." Ahmed turned back to look behind, this time half-standing. "There's something I better tell you. I haven't been completely honest with you. If you turn around, you'll see what I mean. You'll probably be angry."

Donald did not have the energy to turn his head. "What is it?"

But the boy didn't need to say. Donald heard the sound of his name, spoken in Spanish, by his wife. Fiora came around the bank of chairs with her arms open.

VI

She wore one of her light blue pant suits. It bulged out at her stomach, sagged at her breasts, and pushed tight against her thighs. She wore makeup, her black hair in a bun. She carried a small Samsonite suitcase and a Samsonite drug case, as well as her black travel purse.

"Fiora," was all Donald could manage. He looked from her to Ahmed, shocked, betrayed, relieved. When had the boy called her? Sometime earlier in the night. She hated traveling—it was one of the reasons he hadn't wanted her with him in Spain. She disliked makeup, rarely wore the pants suit. She had taken time with all this.

Fiora scolded in Spanish, asked how he was, kissed his forehead, leaving a cool stain of saliva and lipstick behind. She thanked Gil, shaking his hand and taking the tickets from him. He was Gil again, always Gil in her mind. He told her he thought Donald had had at least four Darvon already. She asked where the pills were, and Donald felt her hands rummaging in his pockets.

"I'm not an invalid," he whispered, pushing her hand away. Undaunted, she found the pills and slipped them into her pocket.

"I'm sorry, Donald," the boy said. "I had to do the right thing. I couldn't really care for you. What if something had happened to you? I'm just a guy you met last year. I'm not your family. Allah helped me to see what was right."

"When did he call you, Fiora?"

"At 11:55. I looked at the clock."

"While I was in the park?" Donald asked the boy.

Ahmed nodded. "Then again from Bleecker."

"When had you decided to call her?"

"I kind of decided when I said yes in your study. I was going to tell her out on the balcony while you rested, but I couldn't. I didn't have the guts."

"Donald is a very strong man," Fiora agreed. "He makes people do things."

"I'm glad to see you," Donald told her in Spanish. "But I didn't want you to worry. I wanted to go to Barcelona and come back and relieve you of my burdens for just one week."

She smiled, sitting down next to him. "Men always think that way. There's no logic in it."

"I better go," Ahmed offered. "Are you really going to Spain?" he asked Fiora. "I can help you back to 17th Street."

"We are getting on that plane," Donald assured him. "Don't add sententiousness to betrayal. No one will force me to leave this airport, Fiora."

"We'll go," Fiora told the boy. "I knew that when you called. Donald has been wanting to do this for a long time. Thank you again for the ticket. Are you sure we cannot pay you?"

"What ticket?" asked Donald.

"Ahmed has paid the penalty for changing the ticket to my name, Donaldo. They would not let him change the name on his ticket. He would take no money from me."

Donald shook his head. "You must not pay, Ahmed. We will pay."

"I paid. It's my going-away gift. I'm sorry I can't go with you, Donald. But this is best."

"He has learned compassion from Islam after all," Donald said to his wife in Spanish. "That is the future, Fiora." He raised a weak arm and pointed. "Children of Islam." He said it but felt the rancor slip away with the words, his cheeks warm, his hand reaching out for Fiora's.

"Let the boy be," Fiora said. "You frighten him." She stood up. "Ahmed, thank you. We'll call when we return."

"Okay." They shook hands. Donald didn't offer his hand, but smiled, feeling a little mischief mix in the moment.

"Who is this, Ahmed?" he asked. "Listen carefully: *Ich habe tote, und ich liess sie hin / und war erstaunt sie so getrost zu sehn.*"

"He loves this game," Fiora said to Ahmed. "He plays it even with me, and I never know what he means."

"I don't know German, Donald," the boy reminded him.

"In English, then: 'I have dead ones, and I released them, / amazed to see them so consoled.' Who is that?"

The boy pondered. "Hesse?"

Donald shook his head, waiting.

"I don't know. Who is it?"

"Rilke." Donald smiled. "The poem was his 'Requiem' for his friend. You know what a requiem is, of course."

"Mrs. Fuertes," Ahmed lamented, "he has this idea that if I can't guess his test poems, he will die. I think he's just trying to make me feel guilty. Donald, please don't think things like that."

Donald laughed. "Don't take the words of old men so seriously. No, in fact, perhaps, because you did not guess it, I won't die. Think on that!"

The boy sighed, raising his eyebrows skeptically.

"Take care of yourself, young Mohammed."

"I'll do that," the boy nodded, relieved. "I better go." He raised his hand in a wave. "Thanks for everything, Donald. Sorry about all this. I'll call you in a week."

Donald knew he would not.

"You're a very wonderful young man," Fiora said.

Ahmed thanked her, backed away a little, waving, turning self-consciously. His little black braided ponytail bounced slightly as he walked. He moved through the crowds, looking back once and waving again. Donald watched the boy's back with unmoving eyes, unmoving hands, unmoving lips, pain and exhaustion up his spine, down his legs, through his brain, flowing through his body. The boy turned a corner by a duty-free shop, his skull cap the last thing that disappeared.

Donald squeezed Fiora's hand. "I've been out in the wilderness with that boy," he said. "Thank you for coming."

"Donaldo, you will never escape me. God has bound us."

"That is true." Donald smiled. "You know, Fiora, that Muslim boy drained me of my secrets and my truths and then, like all the young, like youth should be, turned away. I should have seen it coming."

"Tell me what has happened between you, Donaldo?"

"I'll tell you on the plane. We may not hear from him again."

Fiora clicked her tongue. "Of course, we will. We'll write him a postcard from Spain." A young Spaniard across the way pulled out a pocket watch: 4:13. A woman's voice over the loudspeaker called people for boarding. Donald refused the wheelchair, leaned on Fiora's arm instead.

The surprises are all over now, Donald thought as they walked down the tunnel toward the stewardess. We are boarding the plane, and so now the surprises are over. The airplane took off, and they were.

VII

It was a Wednesday in August. Donald and Fiora had been back for a week. The neighbors had all heard about the trip. Donald had wept more at those graves than he thought he could ever weep. Now, they sat in Iglesia de Cristo Pentecostal, on 17th Street, limp with heat. Women fanned themselves with newspapers and hymn pamphlets. Men lifted their hats and wiped their foreheads. Consuela Ramirez stood with Reverend Guillermo at the baptismal pool, confessing her love of Jesus. Wetted, she'd be the only cool person in the house.

Donald heard the splash of her head. He heard nothing else until his left foot shot out in his sleep, banging the back of the next pew. The noise attracted the giggles of children. He dozed again, his eyes opening to commotion, amens, the bustle of bodies. Everyone around him was standing.

"Donaldo, come," Fiora coaxed, her hand gripping his elbow. She guided him out onto the street. Young boys pulled off sweaty shirts and handed them to their mothers, anxious to begin a basketball game. Fiora helped him up the building stairs, through the door, then the kitchen window and onto the fire escape. Donald fell back into a folding chair in exhaustion. He could see down the street by the church some girls joining the boys at their game. Unable to strip down, they pawed at their sweaty shirts and bra lines as the boys kept the basketball from them.

"Are you sure you want to do it?" Fiora asked.

Donald nodded. "Bring the damn thing here, let's get it over with." He sat back, feeling in his pocket the phantom cigarettes he had not smoked in ten years.

Fiora came back out from the kitchen. She held Ahmed's manuscript, a book of matches, and the metal wastebasket from Donald's study. The opus had been waiting at the neighboring Diazvolez flat when Donald and Fiora returned from Spain. No letter, just the manuscript, and *Bismillah Ir Rahaam Ir Raheem* on the manila envelope.

Donald opened the pages to 77. "How," the young man wrote, "shall we reconstruct Western mythology as this century of broken mythologies drags us into self-destruction?"

No small task, Donald thought, no small task. But well left to the young.

He put the manuscript into the bottom of the metal basket, lit a match, and watched with Fiora as the smoke rose up beyond the buildings.

the kapici's wife

Note: In Turkey, kapicis are common to urban apartment buildings. They live with their families in the basements, working as building janitors and caretakers. Because they cannot generally feed their families on the slight pay of a kapici, most hold other jobs as well.

Hakan Karanakci stepped out of his car on Dortuncu Cadde, said goodnight to his driver, and saw in the dusk light something impossible—a prostitute from his teen years, now dressed like a religious village woman, in her baggy *shalvar*, dotted and wrinkled blouse, tight white headscarf, with dirty children on and around her. Emanating from down inside her family's basement apartment was the clangy, Arabesque music of villagers.

The transition staff at the Ministry for Foreign Affairs had moved Hakan's things into the flat a few days ago. He himself had not moved into the apartment until yesterday. Thus, he had not had time to meet the kapici yet, nor this woman, the kapici's wife. Hakan prided himself on having grown beyond most Turkish idiosyncrasies during his years in America, especially fatalism and belief in "Allah's plan." But if this woman were that prostitute, it would be one hell of a coincidence.

The woman stepped out of the entranceway of his building and walked along the side of the building where he couldn't get a good look at her. Since she carried a shopping bag, Hakan figured she would probably cross over to one of the small stores on the east side of the street. He quickly climbed the building's common stairs, unlocked his door, poured himself a Johnnie Walker whiskey, and then opened the window so he could watch her progress. As Hakan waited for her, he easily recalled the scene from fifteen years before.

She had been a naked girl of fifteen, lying open, breasts and body firm, a stained towel near her right arm up at the corner of the bed. She called him "kid," though they were the same age, told him to take his pants off, do his business, and not hold up the line.

"And don't touch my breasts," she said. "I'm young. I don't want everyone ruining them."

The whole room seemed putrid to him, as his grandfather had told him sin rooms would be, stinking of rancid sex, mold, vague fecality. He had gotten his pants down but stood paralyzed. She waited, her hairy groin opening wider. A shot of electricity went through him. He had pulled up his pants, ran out, and sucked in the afternoon air.

Hakan craned his neck further out the penthouse window, but she was not on the street. Dortuncu Cadde, the huge main arterial of the Emek district, serviced dingy apartment buildings, small businesses, honking cars, wild and half-wild cats picking in garbage cans, children screaming their games, street vendors hawking carrots and cucumbers, or buckets, pretzels, old clothes, furniture. Like all of Ankara, it was not relaxing to Hakan, nor interesting. All the housing buildings looked alike, filled with small apartments, the floor of each covered with *kilim* and *hali* carpets, the shelves with copper bowls; all the drinking establishments smelling of licorice-anise *raki;* all the tea houses loud with black-and-white televisions and old men arguing; all the streets inundated with villagers and their children.

Arlington, Virginia, on the other hand, had been wonderfully calm. From his fifteenth-story window, Hakan had been able to

146

see the white dome of the U.S. Capitol building in the distance, the Potomac surrounded by trees, the clean white drape of snow. Louis Armstrong sang "Black and Blue" on the radio, the city and its traffic far off.

There she was!

The kapici's wife came, jostled still by her children, out of the corner grocery store, walking with erect posture under her red-and-orange headscarf. She crossed the street back toward the apartment building. Hakan leaned out the window, calling down to her. She looked around, unable to identify the voice. She walked her children inside. Hakan moved inside his apartment to his front door. Opening it, he could hear the chatter of children below and the slapping of the woman's straw sandals on the basement steps.

"Excuse me, below," he called. "Are you the kapici's wife?"

She stopped. "Yes, I am, beyefendi." She quieted her children.

"May I see you, please? I am the new tenant in the penthouse. I have arrangements concerning my laundry."

"At once, beyefendi," she said. "I'll settle the children downstairs."

Hakan moved back into his flat, leaving the door open so he could hear her coming. He poured himself another whiskey. She would certainly refuse to sit down and talk—she was a married woman alone with an unmarried man not her relation. But she'd want to avoid making the new penthouse tenant angry, especially since he worked for the government.

If this is the girl, Hakan resolved, I must not feel as I always have toward her—inferior, humbled. I must control the . . . he thought of a pun in English . . . the "intercourse" between us.

Her sandals slapped up the stairs. Hakan downed the whiskey, fixed his tie at the mirror, and moved to the center of the room. The woman's somewhat labored breathing preceded her up onto the fifth floor hallway, and Hakan went to his door. Passing a tray of mints on the hall table—he kept them all over the house, one of the first things he'd done upon moving in— he took one, peeled the wrapper, and slipped the smooth candy into his mouth. His hand trembled slightly.

She knocked, pulling her sandals off.

"Please come in," he said. "I am Hakan Karanakci."

"I am Demet," she said, looking at him briefly, then lowering her head.

"Please come in and sit," he said amiably. "I'd like to talk to you."

"You have dirty things. I'd like to take them and go." She had left the door open.

Hakan moved behind her and shut it. He moved to the couch, making himself comfortable. "I've just come back from America. I'm sick of silly Turkish conventions and traditions concerning male/female relations. You probably don't know what I mean, but just believe me. Now sit in that chair, please." His heartbeat quickened. This was definitely the same woman. The oval face, the sad brown eyes, the ripe mouth—older, but all the same.

She came a little farther into the room, stealing a glance back at the door. She was a *sikmabash*, as these women were called, "squeezed heads" because their faces were squeezed into the religious scarf. She didn't wear a traditional gray religious coat, but instead, the iridescent village colors—red and orange like her scarf. Her hands were calloused and, like her wrinkled face, more worn than they ought to be on a woman of thirty. Her clothes were sooty from shoveling coal for the building's heating system. There was black soot under her fingernails and in the lines of her hands.

She frowned and came to the chair. "I can only sit for a moment, beyefendi. I'm sorry to aggravate you." She sat down on the Venetian armchair, keeping her arms close to her sides and hands pressed together on her lap.

"Fine," he nodded. "I have tea prepared. Let me get it."

"No," she exclaimed, jumping up. "I'll get it. Please."

She turned quickly toward the kitchen. There was no sexiness here—nothing but plain self-denial in her baggy hips.

Hakan sat down. He heard her rummaging for spoons in the boxes on the floor. A minute later, she returned with the tea tray.

Hakan lit a cigarette and smiled. "Look at me, Demet. Look at me closely. Do you recognize me from our childhood?"

She shook her head. "I do not. But if we stay here like this together, Hakan Bey, the evil eye will look upon us."

"The evil eye," he chuckled. "I haven't heard from it in years. Do you remember the House of Flame, Demet?"

Now she dropped her head. "I hide nothing from Allah, Hakan Bey. I remember that house, but from another girl's life."

"Does your husband . . . the kapici's name is Ilgaz, I believe?"

"Yes."

"Does he know of this place in Trabzon?"

"Yes," she said.

She must be lying, Hakan thought. He would not have married her if he did. Hakan sat back, blowing smoke rings toward the ceiling. "I've been in a bad mood lately, Demet. I've been drunk. I've been drunk for months. Culture shock is what the psychiatrist calls it. I started getting drunk when I found out I'd been transferred back here to Ankara, this pit. You love it here, of course. Your village was probably poor, like my own childhood home, Ordu. You know Ordu, of course."

"Yes."

"Ankara must be heaven to you." He sighed. "But I hate it here. When did you get to Ankara, by the way?"

"My father and I came eight years ago."

149

"Hmmm. You won't understand, of course, but in America we could have a conversation like this with no discomfort. Freedom and honesty are what human beings need, no matter what our social class. In America everyone firmly believes this. They don't practice it, of course, especially not with the blacks, but they believe it. Has anyone else recognized you, Demet?"

She hesitated, seeming to prepare a "No." She said, "Ankara is far from Trabzon. But there was one man, Hakan Bey. He gave me money and said he would not ruin things for me."

"Very nice of him. He didn't mention anything to your husband?"

"No. But my husband knows everything." She leaned in to pour more tea.

"Of course," Hakan smiled, snuffing out his cigarette in the ashtray, the brown tobacco bursting the paper seams. "Your husband is a generous man. I tell you what we'll do now, Demet. I'm going to describe myself as a boy and you tell me if you remember me—I'm curious. I was small for my age, very vulnerable, my pants down, standing there against the wall. I had almost no private hair. I went to your place because my friends forced me. I wore glasses. Very few village boys wore glasses in those days."

She was already shaking her head. "I'm sorry, Hakan Bey. I do not remember you. I had many boys, but they were all the same boy. I thought I was a bad girl and the boys were sent by Allah to punish me and give me a place in the world. Now I am with Allah and I have a place. I do not remember all the boys."

"I am with Allah." He laughed. "It's been years since I've heard that phrase. 'Allah watches, Allah hears, Allah knows.' My grandfather talked like that. When will people get enough of Allah?"

"Hakan Bey, I'm sorry I make you unhappy. With your permission, I must go. The children will be waiting."

"Demet," Hakan corrected, "you'll stay a little while. I want to talk. Your husband doesn't know you were a prostitute in Trabzon. I *do* know. Just sit a minute."

She wiped her hands on her knees, clasped them tightly on her lap.

"I tell you what." Hakan smiled, conciliatory. "Tell me a few things, then I'll let you go. A meeting like ours, a coincidence like this, should not be wasted. I remember how my grandfather scolded me the evening I went to you, though I think he was proud. He couldn't believe I didn't touch you. He was a strange man. In a way, you were the best thing that happened to me—a silly naked girl there on that creaky bed. You started me away from all those old village ways of thinking and living. I learned English and went overseas and grew beyond my country's provincial beliefs. That's why I never forgot you, I guess. Did I ask you a question? What was I asking you?"

"You have not asked me anything, Hakan Bey."

He frowned, trying to remember. The whiskey was addling his thoughts. "I know what it was: How did you become a prostitute? My friends and I always made up big tales about you girls."

She looked down at her hands. "It was a long time ago, Hakan Bey. My father left Trabzon to go to Van where there was work. My sister was seventeen and I was fourteen, and we had no money. The aunt who took care of us didn't care about us. My mother was dead. We needed money to live. A friend of my sister's friend knew how to make money. I only thought I would do it for a little while. I told the men to touch me as little as possible."

"'Don't touch my breasts,' you said. I remember that. And then what?" Underneath the soot and drooped eyes and slight smell of basement living, Hakan saw the young prostitute again.

It was as if he sat there as two men—one repulsed by the dirty villager in front of him, the other stirred to the loins.

"I was pregnant twice," Demet hesitated. "There maybe was a third time, but I got scraped twice. It was very bad. We worked for nothing. All the money we worked for went to our 'uncle.' We hated him. My father came from Van one day and took me back to Ordu. He was crazy and beat me with the stick he used on the donkey. I became very sick with an infection from a cut." She pointed to behind her right knee, rubbing it. "I cried from bruises and welts until I couldn't move. My father believed I was sick and didn't hit me anymore. He washed and nursed me like a woman. He prayed for me."

She had raised her head, looking away from Hakan toward the open window and the sounds of the street, the hard skin of the poor in her face.

"And religion?" Hakan pressed her. "How did you become a *sikmabash*?"

She lowered her head again, studying her calloused hands. "When my sickness was gone, women came to me again. Giril Hanim came. She was a nice woman whose husband died. She taught me about Allah and the Quran. When she died, my father brought me to Ankara, where my mother's sister lived with her family. They are very religious. I have not thought dirty thoughts in many years."

She raised her eyes. "I have told it to you as I told the other man. Please do not mention these things to my husband, Hakan Bey. It would become very bad for me."

Yes, it would, Hakan thought, closing his eyes.

He had expected to take out pent-up anger on her. He had felt it for years, after the humiliation of running away from her. But now he just felt numb. And her quaint tale of village life was like one of those cliché village films that were so popular. You didn't want to watch the sentimental tripe, but when you did, they always jerked a tear out of you. He had wanted something from this woman . . . what had he wanted?

"May I go now, Hakan Bey?"

"In a minute," Hakan said. "Let me ask you something. Fifteen years ago, you were a prostitute. I paid you money and never got to screw you. You don't remember it, but I do. Now, fifteen years later, if I told your husband what I know, he would leave you. So now, fifteen years later, I will ask you a question: If, right now, I told you to raise your skirts and lie on my bed, what would you do?"

She thought only a moment, as if she'd been expecting the question. "I cannot lose my husband. But please do not ask it. The other man did not ask it."

Hakan waved away her distress with his hand. "I won't ask it, Demet. But it's amazing how you remind me of it all. The village. The wretched life. So much shame. I'm thinking of my grandfather. He came to our village of Esbiye from Uzbekistan and never went back. He didn't worry over protocols. If he had met you like this fifteen years later, he would have forced you into sex and not thought twice. He didn't care for good manners or guilt or looking back with regret. People are not strong like that anymore. The West has softened me, he would say."

Hakan stood up, and Demet immediately stood as well.

"I talk too much," Hakan said. "Take some mints for your children." He reached one for himself out of the mint tray on the coffee table.

"No, thank you, Hakan Bey."

Hakan lifted the tray. "I asked you to take some to your children."

She reached in quickly, took a few, and dropped them like coins into her *shalvar* pocket.

153

"Come for my laundry on Saturdays," Hakan said. "That's tomorrow, isn't it. Well, come tomorrow for it. I'll have some. And I will not keep you this long in the future."

"I will come," she nodded. She waited a split second to be dismissed. When he said nothing, her urge to escape overwhelmed decorum. She hurried to the door, opened it, put her sandals back on, then closed the door softly behind her.

This is home, Hakan thought. Get used to it, as the Americans would say. The sound of Demet's quick footsteps, muted by the closed door, faded away. Why had he thought, two weeks ago, packing up in Arlington, things would have changed back here? Nothing had changed. Prostitutes were still turning religious and, presumably, the religious were becoming prostitutes; villagers still flocked into cities which only gave them menial lives; whole cities all over the Mideast were jerry-built just to keep up with Europe and America; and Grandfather's Allah still played tricks whereby a prostitute from a village years ago appeared in Ankara.

Hakan moved to the window, the feeling of mint in his mouth like a soft burning. The smell of the kapici's wife was still in the air as he passed her chair, a smell of unbathed soot and sweat and village life a hundred mints could not efface. Hakan pushed the window open as far as it would go until it jutted perpendicular to the building. He leaned out, breathing in the coal-soaked Ankara air.

II

The hint of a sound came to her. She had fallen asleep while Ibrahim, the baby, nursed. Her husband slept on the chair against the wall, his mouth open, snoring softly. She awoke to the sweet feeling of an emptied breast restoring itself, already, with warmth. Ibrahim, just about one, still pursed his lips to suck. He lay on her with the lips pursed, though he slept. Demet saw from the Syrian wall clock, her mother-in-law's wedding gift, that it was twelve-thirty. She had only been asleep for about twenty-five minutes.

What was that sound?

Demet looked over at her husband's thick chest and muscled stomach, naked and undulating. The poor Hakan from upstairs—the drunk man who could cause such trouble—he seemed almost womanly: fair-skinned, probably hairless at the chest, hands without calluses. How could he remember fifteen years ago? She remembered nothing. It was wrong to remember individual boys, so she did not. Would Hakan Bey want sex now? Men wanted sex. They wanted the mouth. Could she give the mouth? Would he be quiet if she did? Would the mouth be enough?

Demet felt a tear form in her left eye and clutched her baby. No matter what, there would be disgrace again. Hakan Bey would force her to his room more than once, and then one day, neighbors—Fatima Hanim in 4B or Serpil Hanim in 3C—would wonder to each other why Demet, mother of three, the lowly kapici's wife, visited the penthouse at awkward times. There were no secrets here. If she told her husband the truth about her past, he would turn away from her, maybe beat her, though he never had before. He would take the children to his mother. Divorce would be quick. She had married him without telling him about her past. It was not illegal, she did not think, for her to have done this—but the judge would see her sin. She would be left with nothing. It was not enough that Allah knew her secret. Everyone would know.

Closing her eyes, Demet thought of her wedding night—the rose water and her own blood from a prick under the big toe, the old trick for fooling drunk newlywed husbands, and their mothers. Ilgaz, big hairy Ilgaz, who did not love her but knew a man's duty to care for his family like a lion, was fooled by her tears of pain on her wedding night.

"I'm sorry," he groaned, hard and large in her hole that had been virginal since she found Allah five years before. He pushed and groaned and then spent himself. She had cried tears and surreptitiously let out the tiny bag of blood, kept warm under her shirt—which he would never take off her, a proper man— keeping the blood clear of his body part, in case it was cooler yet than new blood. He had rolled off her, glancing down to the blood—warned to do so by his mother—then he looked away and turned off the bedside lamp.

Demet remembered that night clearly but remembered the other boys and men only like dreams. Because dreams never happened, how could they be remembered for long? They were not even a leaf on a tree. They were a shadow, and shadows disappeared.

The sound again. Something just outside by the daylight window, moving on the ground. A cat?

Demet rose, closing her gown completely, carrying her sleeping baby. She tiptoed to the window. If it was a dog bothering the ground and Ilgaz awoke, he would try to kill it. Dogs were good food, even if stringy. He knew Demet's love of little animals, but he would not give up food for his family. Demet pulled the curtain back quietly. She peered into night air lit only by a distant light from the building's south pathway. She saw nothing. The dog or cat was gone.

Demet wiped her eyes and returned to bed. Silently, she murmured parts of the second Surah as the covers warmed her and her baby again. She was cold, as always, but Ilgaz ran so hot—she sleeping in gown and blankets, and he half naked.

Demet envied men some things, including how hot their bodies ran, like beings on fire. But she did not ever want to be a man. Men needed so much help from deep within—like the drunk, Hakan. They were not solid, and their minds played tricks. A woman could be forced to do anything, this was true—but from force of evil or of men, not from their own weakness. Even in Allah's grace, men were still weak, still full of temptations. It was women who, with Allah's grace, became the strong ones. Allah, Demet knew, would keep her strong and help her find a way to keep Hakan Bey from letting his weakness ruin her life.

The warm bed gave her hope. "Yes," she thought, "Allah's will is strong in me. Allah will show me a way. Allah is my father and my mother. I am loved by Allah, like no human can love me.

"Allah, all merciful, all powerful, I am your servant. I suffer for you. Help me, Allah."

Demet lay beside her sleeping baby and prayed into the night. By the time sleep came again, she felt a return of paradise in her breathing and knew, as if watching branches blown back in a huge wind, that Allah was near.

She was not surprised when she woke with a start around three-thirty a.m. Allah touched her with carnelian, a whisper in her ear.

She knew exactly what to do.

III

Hakan had already put his laundry in the living room when Demet knocked on his door in the late morning.

"Come in, Demet," he said, and she padded in two steps, leaving the door open. Though her head was lowered, ensconced in another red-orange scarf, he saw that her face was pale, as if she had slept badly. He himself had a headache, dry mouth, and a sore elbow. He could not remember most of the night before, but he knew he had gone to the chai house, played backgammon, drunk raki, then found a bar for some real whiskey. He remembered nothing after that, but he must have fallen somewhere, because his jacket and pants were dirty and slightly torn. He saw no blood anywhere, and he felt no soreness, except the elbow. He assumed that he had not fought with anyone or fallen too badly.

"The laundry is there," he pointed, yawning. He wished the aspirin would kick in harder, and the coffee. Why didn't the woman just take the laundry and go?

"Hakan Bey," Demet said meekly.

"What is it?"

She kept her head lowered but closed the door behind her.

"I have diseases," she said, looking up at him now, with no humble avoidance of his eyes as would be appropriate. She had a cold sore at the corner of her mouth. He hadn't noticed it yesterday. "I have venereal diseases from some of the boys . . . back then . . . in Trabzon." She touched her cold sore, "Anyone I have sex with, or sex with my mouth, they become sick too. Forever. Like me."

Hakan found himself speechless. She was brave to tell him this. But of course, she had a purpose—to keep him at bay. She still thought herself attractive enough for him? Or was she just scared? Interesting. After yesterday, he'd felt no inclination to bring up the past again, certainly not in any sexual way. But perhaps he should have thought about it. She wasn't so bad looking.

But no. What a way to think. It would be crass to even think of her sexually.

The West has changed me, Hakan thought, shaking his head. I feel compassion for this woman. And morality? Did that come from the West? No, that came from right here.

"I am an unhappy man, Demet Hanim," he said, purposefully using the suffix of respect for a married woman. "I believe I am what is called 'depressed.' I drink too much. I am divorced. There was . . . an event. In America, marriages end every minute." Demet was looking again at her feet. "But Demet—look at me. Look at my eyes."

She found him again with her hazel eyes.

"I'm actually a man of honor. Believe it or not, I will not betray your secret. Do you see that? You need not worry."

She nodded.

Did she really have VD, he wondered. Probably not. That sore wasn't there yesterday. Was she courageous in coming up here, or stupid?

Hakan walked to his liquor cart, poured a Johnnie Walker straight. He downed the whiskey, then refilled his glass. "Do you read?" he asked, turning to her. She had not moved, knowing she was not yet dismissed—trying to think of how else to convince him to stay away from her.

"The *Tao Te Ching*." He laughed. "Have you heard of it?"

He did not wait for an answer. Nancy had loved reading ancient "Eastern" philosophy. To her, Islam was not East, Mecca was not East—China was.

"America, I discovered, is actually farther east than Turkey—did you know that?" He chuckled, though she would have no idea why. He picked up the gray-white illustrated English translation he had been reading for the last few weeks, as if it would help. Or perhaps he read it just to remember Nancy?

"Oh yes, Demet, the Americans believe in many things Eastern—at least the educated like to dabble in the 'East.' My wife—my ex-wife—gave me this as a gift last Christmas. I hate to admit it, but she understood my kind of honor."

Hakan sensed the alcohol—the fresh edge of it, sweet, buzzing. Demet seemed to stare, "caught in the headlights," as the Americans said. How powerless she really was. How sad. How real.

"Accept disgrace willingly," Hakan read, trying to carry a bit of flourish. "Accept misfortune as the human condition. Accept being unimportant."

He paused, looking up. Her hands were folded in front of her, her head down, the damn red-orange scarf so colorful on such a drab life.

"That's us, Demet. Unimportant. I'll bet you accept it better than me. Do not be concerned with loss or gain. This is called 'accepting disgrace willingly.'"

Hakan raised his eyes again to Demet. She understood nothing, ironically. She who really knew disgrace.

"You've been courageous to tell me your secrets, Demet Hanim. What I am saying to you now is that I will keep them, just as you will keep any secrets you know of me. Go now. Take my wash and go."

Nancy used to like doing laundry. "It's an intimacy women get to have," she had said. A WASP woman from Connecticut, she was like every American woman—she wanted domesticity and yet she wanted to ascend to the top of the corporate ladder too. At first, she had thought Hakan could give her both—he was traditional, but malleable enough. He was not his Quran-toting grandfather. He enjoyed her passion for the law and her law practice. He secretly believed that when children came, she would give up the law or at least most of her practice, but until then, they could be passionate, high-living lovers.

But he was a drunk. A stupid drunk. America was now lost

to him. The Turkish government had brought him home—to be changed back into who he had been?

Demet bent for the laundry, lifted the bag, and slung it over her shoulder. She slipped into her flattened shoes and stepped out, closing the door behind her. Hakan poured himself another whiskey and tossed the *Tao* toward the wastebasket, missing by a few inches. It hit the floor with a loud bang, which throbbed in his head.

"I'm lost," he said aloud. "What will I do?" The answer was back in America, he sensed—more a longing than logic, for Hakan knew that he was not in America; he was here, in Emek, returned to the land he had fled, with no way out for the foreseeable future.

Hakan shook himself head to toes, like a dog after a bath. He moved toward the window, wondering about his professional future—he was a hair's breadth from suspension—and searching his drunken memory for good times in his Turkish past. Through the open window he smelled the dry, sooty air, and heard car horns. Children played hopscotch in the grass and dirt in front of the adjacent building. The smell of exhaust from the street, the cries of vendors, the screaming of children and honking of cars rose up to him.

"Culture shock," the ministry's psychiatrist, a wiry, fifty-plus bespectacled man, had called it. "It will hit you hard." Hakan Karanakci, Assistant to the Cultural Attaché, had assured the overworked civil servant that he would stop drinking, he would get help, he would take advantage of the government program. He had not really believed the psychiatrist about the severity of the illness, but now, after two days on Dortuncu Cadde, he knew better.

Hakan closed his eyes, his ears buzzing, the noise of the street like the sound of locomotion in his head.

This was more than culture shock. It was the numbing loneliness of coming home. Hakan knew himself as a man of honor, but he thought of Demet again, and wondered how drunk he would have to become to go after her, learn the truth about her disease, and then if she turned out to have been lying, turn her into a whore again.

The possibility of this scene was not so far off for him as he watched the street, downed the whiskey, and then raised the glass again for any last drop of its particular soothing, sweet, and warm blood. Perhaps I'll wait to see if she comes out the building's front door again, like yesterday afternoon. Perhaps I'll let her know that I am watching.

Hakan was vaguely aware of feeling disgrace as he pictured Demet naked in his living room, but he also felt that nothing else, at this time, seemed so thrilling.

And he was acutely aware of wanting another drink. Rubbing his slightly bruised elbow, he pushed up off the window edge, turned back into his flat, and returned to the liquor cart. He spied the wall clock: It was not even eleven a.m. He poured himself another drink.

civilizations are islands

The other two adults at the dinner table, Aunt Nura and Uncle Ahmed, were already groaning with cynicism. Katrina, thirteen, didn't quite understand why they groaned, but since her mother was the object of their derision, Katrina joined in. She set her fork down onto her plate of shawarma lamb and curled up her nose.

"Oh, Sadia." Aunt Nura frowned. "You love saying the huge things. The world watch out now that you've decided to go back to your writing."

"Civilizations are just islands in a sea of barbarism." That's what her mother had said. Somehow, she was referring to how uncivilized people—like Papa—behaved, and somehow she was saying that civilization had no real effect on people like Papa. Or something like this. Her mother's conversations had been wandering ones since she'd packed up the house in Delhi. She'd been so tired and sad these last few days, coming home to Egypt to start a new life without a husband—ready for the shame of divorce in a Muslim world, but also for freedom from his physical abuse. Papa only hit Katrina sometimes, but he hit Mama lots more. He was an American, so Katrina was half American too. She loved him, loved how he danced with her, how he played music on his clarinet, trumpet, drums. He could play any instrument. She did not mind that he had never taken her to America. She didn't mind that he paid most of his attention to Indian music gurus and his university colleagues.

But when he hit Mama, Katrina felt scared and angry. She hated the fear, and she hated the shame of being afraid. She wished she was a boy and could hit him back hard enough to knock him out. On her mother's right cheekbone right now was a bruise, half hidden by makeup, three days old. Katrina remembered vividly her father slapping her mother in the kitchen in Chandigarh on Sunday.

Katrina dropped her head, missing India—a country with fifteen official languages, a billion warring peoples, everywhere a guru or astrologer or Brahman for sale. Katrina's mother had told her on the plane ride to Egypt, "You'll hate all adults for a while, especially me. But I'm all you've got now—you'll have to control yourself. You'll have to be civilized."

As the airplane left Cairo for Aswan, Katrina closed her eyes and imagined her mother drop out the window. Pushing mother out certainly hadn't been the "civilized" thing to do! Her mother tumbled off the plane's wing and fell down toward the pyramids. The point of a pyramid parted, then closed again. The desert accepted the body. Papa took Mama's place in the airplane seat next to Katrina. Why was that? Why didn't Katrina hate him more? Katrina wiped her mouth with her napkin, aware that she felt too many things at once, and that they didn't make any sense.

"I hope they're more than islands," Aunt Nura said. "Fatalism is that oriental death our parents taught you and me, the new Egyptians, to avoid. If I thought that after all your troubles you're bowing to fatalism, I would fear for you. You'll become one of those fatalist writers, so sentimental. There has to be more for you—higher purpose now—than to say, all is Fate and I'm flotsam. Why not say: I'm free of my old fate!"

Mama was a pretty woman, despite the bruise—her skin a light brown, her earrings always in blues and sapphires, her eyes a rich brown, so that they showed in her lighter face like jewels against a beige backdrop, her black hair down below her shoulders, with tiny gossamer streaks of gray starting near the roots at the crown of her head.

Sighing, she now neglected her beauty for sternness, putting her napkin to her lips, then dropping it back onto her lap.

Mama said, "Nura, you bow to your cooking, to your commute, to your work, to the dust of the desert, to the exhaust fumes and horns, to your husband's demands, to your crazy governments, to assassinations and conflagrations. You bow to your life of Muslim tradition and North African habit and, on top of all that, you know at any moment, through no cause or effect of your own, your life can end. Maybe a bomb, maybe a car wreck, maybe cancer. Everything is fragile. Even the Westernization of Egypt. It's fragile too. Egypt could soon be consumed by war, or by silly Western values, or by silly Islam. You know how fragile life is, Nura, yet you have chosen your fatalism—you strive to see the sun rise out of the West. Why? Because you have hitched your fate there. We're all fatalists. At least I admit it."

What were these women talking about? Katrina thought. After all that had happened, why did they talk about things so abstract?

"Sadia!" Nura cried. "When in God's name did you become so cynical? Fifteen years with that Negro communist must have done it. I'm keeping you here in my house for as long as it takes to accomplish a little perestroika. No more of this thinking in the extremes."

"I'm going for a walk," Katrina interrupted.

"It's too late in the evening," her mother said, setting her fork down.

"Oh, let her go, Sadia," Aunt Nura said, touching Katrina's arm. "She'll be fine. We can keep arguing and not bore her. You're too intelligent for all this, aren't you, Katrina?"

"What if I just go downstairs and visit Fatih?" Katrina counter-offered, without answering her aunt.

"Fine." Her mother nodded. "Just stay in the building."

How bizarre, Katrina thought. You could love a mother and hate her at the same time. Katrina thought suddenly of a teddy bear her father had sent away for when she was about five, an American Winnie-the-Pooh. How bizarre to miss it suddenly, at thirteen. How stupid.

Katrina took her plate to the kitchen. She saw herself reflected in the dark window over the sink. She took after her father: handsome, black, with kinky hair and a temper that was always ready to burst. If not for her mother's calmer blood, she would have been in a hundred fistfights in school.

"You're so much like your father sometimes," her mother said. "It scares me." But her breasts, jutting out into the small bra, her first period, and pubic hair coming at eleven—she was undeniably becoming a woman. In India and in Egypt, many girls were getting married at thirteen, possessed completely by the family of women around them, women bending over them, waxing their pubic hair, instructing them, preparing them. If her father hadn't been an expatriate, atheist, communist American and her mother not a Westernized Egyptian—educated in Chicago, where she met Papa—Katrina might be a wife already, her body covered in layers of clothing.

Katrina let herself out of the apartment and descended the staircase toward Fatih's flat. Would Fatih already have told all of Aswan about the "change" in Katrina's family? Would everyone know her parents were getting divorced? Fatih had a big mouth. Katrina wasn't even sure why she had said she wanted to see Fatih—it had simply been the first idea that had come to her. Maybe the girl, two years younger than Katrina, wouldn't even be home. But if that were so, Katrina would have to go back up to the grown-ups. Katrina's life as she'd known it was over. Her Indian friends, like her girlfriend Jahiri, out of her life forever. Her family a matter of shame, her adolescence sent into an alien land as she returned with her mother to this Muslim country permanently, this country she had visited more than once with her parents, but found, compared to India, squalorous and uninteresting. In the midst of all this, the adults upstairs were carrying on some worthless, intellectual dinner-table discussion. Katrina could kill herself and no one would notice.

II

"Hello, Katrina," Fatih's mother smiled. Was it a smile of judgment and condescension? "Fatih has gone across to the village for the evening."

Katrina made small talk with her, and soon the door closed. Fatih had gone to visit her cousin in the Nubian village across the river. That was all right. Katrina could find her there. It beat going back upstairs, and there might even be a little adventure in it. She looked at her watch—7:30. Her father was known in the village—he had helped bring American jazz musicians for Nubian music festivals. Katrina herself hadn't been there in years. People wouldn't recognize her. She could just find Fatih, maybe walk along the river and make fun of the tourists in her mind—stupid Americans, most of them, getting fleeced by the taxi and *felucca* drivers.

She went down the remaining three flights of stairs and out the front door. The chill of the evening breeze hit her immediately, and she rubbed at her thinly sleeved arms. The air would be even colder on the *felucca* ride across the river. But she certainly couldn't go back upstairs and get her coat. Her mother would forbid her to go across the river alone. But there was another problem: her thin white shirt. The bra showed through it, and she wore no head scarf. This wouldn't be liked in the village.

Should she risk it? On the quick walk down the dimly lit Abbas Farid Street toward the well-lit Corniche, she decided that if things went easily, she'd go across. If not, she'd come back home. Let fate decide, she thought, mocking her mother and aunt in her mind. If she got across, she could borrow a sweater and scarf from Fatih's cousin. She could borrow some nice tourist's jacket on the *felucca* ride. It was January, and tourists were always taking cool evening rides.

Under the streetlights and amid the bustle of people along the boardwalk, Katrina forgot the cold a little. She walked to Abu Simbel Hotel, crossed the street, came to the concrete steps that descended to the Nile.

An old wizened black-as-night *felucca* captain sitting on a ledge and smoking a cigarette called out in Arabic, "Young woman, where you going so naked?" She ran quickly down the steps to where an American couple in their sixties or seventies and a Nubian were engaged in monetary sign language.

"Can I help you folks?" she asked, calming her breath. She greeted the Nubian in Arabic and bowed her head slightly.

"He speaks nothing but Arabic or Nubian," the skinny elderly woman said. "We want to go over across the river to the Botanical Gardens."

"He understands that much," her husband said. "It's the price we can't settle on."

"How much did he ask?" Katrina smiled kindly. Be nice to these Americans, she thought, and they'll help me get to my destination. Maybe ask them what America was like on the way? Or just pretend she already knew.

"He wants thirty pounds."

"It's too much. If I get him down to twenty, will you give me a ride across to the village?"

"Well, I don't see why not."

Twenty was still too much, but no one would be the worse for it. The captain, who would make a killing, might feel enough gratitude not to ask questions about Katrina's clothing or the fact that she was out at evening alone.

The captain accepted the price but did not thank her for her assistance. Clearly disgusted at her lack of clothing, he glared at Katrina as he pushed them off the shore and then sat in the back of the *felucca*, guiding it and trying to listen to them talk.

The Americans wanted to know everything about their "little angel." The man, Jim, lent her his jacket. She told them she was going to meet her father, a music teacher, in the village. He would be at the house of a singer named Hafi. She told them she hadn't been to the village in five years. Everything, except her father's presence, was true enough.

The trip took just under a half hour. When they arrived at the other shore, she said goodbyes and jumped out quickly. As she started up toward the village, she heard Jim comment that she was "so regal and mature for a young girl." Americans talked as if they wanted to be overheard, or didn't care, or just didn't realize how voices can carry over the Nile. Katrina felt a pang of desire to see her father, brought on by Jim's American accent.

When she had visited this village with her father before, he had left her one time at the house of a huge, nameless woman on the outskirts of town. The woman hadn't really enjoyed baby-sitting an eight-year-old girl who spoke no Nubian, but she had been hospitable enough. Katrina paused now in front of the house, which had changed very little in five years, except that a male must have made the pilgrimage to Mecca and then returned to paint the doorway and front wall a mural of animals, mosques, and trees.

Katrina heard voices inside an open window and moved on. As she passed a well-lit, silent adobe home, she tried to remember where her father's friend, Hafi, lived. She walked up to a window, peeked under the edge of a curtain at a typical village home—a girl about her age going into a back room, a half-naked child scratching his backside, an older woman teaching another girl some embroidery.

Katrina avoided the mud in the road and walked past the schoolhouse. The village was like so many others in both Egypt and India. The houses were small and rectangular, made from adobe or concrete, light emanating from behind thinly curtained windows, dogs barking, little scratches of sound here and there, and the constant smell of mud. Most of the men would be in the tea house or at a friend's place, playing cards, talking, watching one of the village's only televisions. The townspeople were too conservative to allow much drinking, but the men would act drunk, like men talking together at night always acted, gesturing more severely than necessary.

Some children squatted with a mother and an older sister in a doorway as she passed. Katrina nodded to them, felt their eyes on her back. Some older children looked out a window at a soccer game up the street where four boys kicked a half-flat basketball. Katrina recognized no one around her. She attracted stares from the boys, but they returned to their game after she passed.

Rounding a corner, she stopped short. She thought she had just heard her father's laugh. She jerked her head toward the house she had just passed. Two children at a nearby window craned to look there with her.

"Who lives in there?" she asked in Arabic, hoping they spoke it.

"Uncle Abdul and the family," the older boy said in competent Arabic.

Then the laugh came again, but now the man's voice jabbered in Nubian. Her father knew Arabic but very little Nubian.

"Do you children know Fatih from Aswan?" she asked.

"Uncle Mahmoud's niece?"

"Yes. Do you know where I can find her?"

The boy considered her for a moment then nodded. "I'll show you where she is."

For the first time since she left Aswan to cross the river, Katrina realized the wildness of what she was doing—a girl, half-clothed, walking alone in this Nubian village. It thrilled her. Now the boy from the window came out of the house. He was about eight years old, tall and shirtless. He said, "Big sister, you should cover your head in this village, unless you're a tourist. Your girlfriend will give you a scarf."

"And you should live in Iran." Katrina laughed. "I wasn't aware that Egypt had accepted *Sharia* law." The boy hurried in front of her. She caught up to him, determined to match his stride.

"Little brother," she said, "you are so poorly educated, you think Allah will punish me for not wearing a scarf. That's what you think, don't you?"

"Allah has punished you already," he shrugged. "You're traveling with no coat and no friends." The boy pointed to a house where a girl of about three was waving at him. "Take big sister to Fatih," he called to her.

Katrina felt an overwhelming urge to slap his supercilious little face. Her father would have hit the boy; or at least he would have hit something. The boy looked at her peacefully, expecting thanks. She stood frozen for a moment, feeling her throat pumping blood, her fists clenching. But somewhere in it all, a spark of reason shot up. She was in a strange village and didn't belong.

She muttered her thanks. The little girl came up to her and offered her hand. Katrina took it, turned away from the boy, blowing out her breath angrily, and followed her new little friend into the house.

III

She stood, stared at, in a crowd of village women. After a look of terrible surprise, Fatih had hugged her and introduced her to all the women. The room was small, paint peeling where chairs scraped against the walls. The women sat on a couch, hard chairs, and floor cushions, pondering her. It was obvious that they knew everything about the divorce already. "So, *this* is the poor girl," their pitying faces said. "This is the daughter of that American man who leaves his family for another woman." They wouldn't know that he hit his wife and daughter, and most wouldn't have thought that a terrible sin. Katrina knew you didn't tell women like this the truth about men because they often blamed the women.

When Fatih took her to a side room to find a sweater and scarf, Katrina was so angry she could barely speak. "How could you tell them about the divorce?" she hissed.

Three children lay asleep on a bed, a boy breathing loudly in the semi-darkness. Fatih pulled a shawl out from under his legs and he sighed, turning over.

"I didn't expect you to come here," Fatih whispered, adding quickly, "but I'm really glad you came."

Katrina grabbed Fatih by the arm. "I knew you'd tell everyone. You can't keep your mouth shut."

"Ouch!" Fatih pulled away. "You're hurting me!" Katrina hadn't noticed how hard she was gripping Fatih's arm. "I wouldn't have told them if I knew you were coming. You hate it over here. Why did you come?"

"I just did, that's all. I don't like all these women staring at me."

"They're not staring. Anyway, I can't believe your parents are getting a divorce. If mine did, I'd die."

"My parents have ruined my life. I hope they go to hell."

They had come back into the room of women, and one at the door must have heard.

"Who are you sending to hell, little sister?" she asked from behind thick glasses.

"No one," Katrina said, feeling her stomach knot.

"It must be someone," the woman said. "Hell is not empty."

"No one."

The women wore black modesty gowns and headscarves. All but one was black Nubian. They sat knitting, sewing, talking, drinking tea. Some girls Katrina's age and just older were dressed more colorfully, but still modestly—no pants, all blouses double-layered and all heads covered with *hijabs*. Katrina counted ten women and six girls, all crowded into a room with no paintings on the walls, no bookshelves, no hangings. The floors were covered with carpets, many quite worn.

"She's a pretty enough girl," said a woman who sat knitting, her needles clicking with a machine's quickness. "But she has a foul mouth. What's your name, girl?"

"Katrina."

"Your mother's Egyptian, isn't she?"

"My mother's Egyptian and my father's American."

"Isn't your father used to come visit Uncle Hafi?" another woman asked in awkward Arabic.

"Yes."

"Spoke Nubian terrible. Said his slave grandparents were upper Nile Valley."

"They were from here, yes, many generations ago."

"Maybe a Nubian woman could control him. Your mother can't."

The one at the door said, "I still want to know who she's sending to hell in my husband's house."

What stupid women! Katrina thought. Why were women in the world anyway? They gossiped and knitted and let things happen to them. And it was dumb to freeze on the river just to come over here to be stared at by a bunch of village women. Katrina could see them all machine-gunned to death—she herself held the machine gun.

The woman by the door got up, put her knitting on her chair, and came over. She squatted, her knees popping, her face now lower than Katrina's. The woman's nose was huge, and she had a big mole with shoots of hair just above her lips.

"You must feel pretty unhappy these days," the woman said, "to run away over here without your mother and without any clothes."

"I didn't run away," Katrina said. "What are you talking about? And I don't need my mother to come across the river. I'm not a girl anymore."

This brought some low laughter. The squatting woman raised her hand and Katrina flinched. But the hand merely shushed the women.

"I won't hit you," the woman said.

"Her daddy hits her all the time," Fatih said. "She was in the hospital once."

"Fatih!" No one was supposed to know that. Katrina never admitted it.

"Well, she must have deserved it," another woman said. "She's a sour girl."

The squatting woman put her hand on Katrina's shoulder and pushed herself up. Her knees popped again. "We should get this girl home to her mother," she said. "She lives in your building, Fatih?"

"Yes, she's staying with her aunt."

The fat woman turned to a girl about eleven with a long, dark braid. "Nadia, go find Ibrahim and tell him he'll take you girls back across. This girl's mother must be worried."

Nadia opened the door and stepped out.

"She won't be worried," Katrina murmured. "She doesn't care about me." Even as the words came out, Katrina heard how childish they sounded. How stupid she made herself sound.

"That girl deserves more than a beating," said the woman with the thick glasses. "I should give her one myself, talking about her mother that way, after she been through."

"It's alright," the woman with the mole soothed. "She's just a confused girl."

Fatih wouldn't let it go. "She told me once that she hated her mother. She wants to be like her father. Didn't you, Katrina?"

"Is that true?" the kind woman asked.

Katrina closed her eyes. "Be quiet, Fatih!" she hissed, clenching her fists. She felt tears coming. She would hate herself if she cried like a little girl.

"You've had a hard time, haven't you?" the woman said, taking Katrina's shoulder and leading her to two chairs by the door. The woman picked up her knitting, and they both sat down.

"If you hate your mother," the woman told Katrina gently, "you hate yourself. You have no choice about who you are, little sister. We women stick together no matter what. A grown-up girl knows that."

Katrina lowered her head. No matter what happened, no matter even the kindness of this woman, Katrina felt ashamed and angry. That was all there had been in her for days now. It seemed like that was all there would ever be. No matter whether she was on a plane, or on a street, or in a flat, or in this village, she felt like everyone just wanted to look at her. Katrina froze. Indeed, she realized, everyone was looking at her. For a second, all she could think was that maybe her mother would come in the door and rescue her.

The room was silent except for water steaming up from a pot, the clicking of needles, a sigh—then the door scraped open. Nadia came in and said Ibrahim was ready to take them.

Katrina closed her eyes again. Maybe if she sat there long enough with her eyes closed, everyone would disappear. It would be like whiteness, like the Englishwoman, Gayle, the woman who taught piano in her father's music department at the university, a very white woman. She could go to someplace like London and be invisible among the people there.

"Come on, little sister." The woman put her hand under Katrina's arm, pulling upward.

Katrina opened her eyes, stood, her eyes down, avoiding the eyes all around her. The woman by the fire who spoke badly, the slumped old woman next to her, the little girls playing with a wad of wool—all of them looked at her like they would look at an ant.

Katrina turned away from them toward the door. If she had been a man, or even just a grown woman, these women wouldn't have treated her this way. Even if she had been a tourist, they wouldn't have. But they considered her a child because she had acted like a child, jumping on a sailboat, crossing the river in just a shirt when she knew it was wrong, trusting in Fatih's discretion when Fatih was just a child.

Katrina said nothing to Fatih during the boat ride back, not even when Fatih began to cry. On the Aswan side, she left Fatih and sat at a table in the Abu Simbel Hotel garden until a waiter told her to leave. She walked back to Aunt Nura's building, unsure of which she wanted to blow up more, the Nubian village or herself.

IV

Her mother had her blouse off. Her breasts sagged in a flesh-colored bra. She was being very nice about Katrina's disappearance, especially after Katrina had come in and wept in her arms.

"I hate everyone!" she confessed to her mother. "I hate Papa, I hate you, I hate . . ." Her mother held her in swan's wings and murmured to her and did not let go, even when the crying stopped, and Katrina tried to speak but could not.

"I don't know if I can be civilized and live in Aswan," Katrina finally murmured, as her mother let her go and they sat together on the edge of the bed.

"You have no choice," her mother said, practical now, standing to move to the bathroom.

Katrina used the toilet, wiped herself, then came beside her mother at the mirror. Her mother applied face cream, covering the bruise on her cheek for a second then, the cream absorbed by skin, revealing it. Katrina fingered the yellowish-white cream in a wide, round bottle. Applying his shaving cream, her father always said, "White products made *by* white people *for* white people."

"How did I get to be so black?" she muttered to her mother in the mirror. "I think I'm black on the outside," Katrina told her, "but not on the inside."

Her mother said nothing, pulled her skirt up, and sat on the toilet. Her urine dropped like a waterfall into the basin. Katrina took her shirt then bra off, scratched a small breast, then pulled on her nightshirt—long, beige, with little saxophones all over it.

"I'm sorry you feel so alone here," her mother said as they walked back into the bedroom. Her mother removed her bra and took her nightgown off the back of the chair. "You have a lot of bad feelings, but you've held your temper very well. You even held it with those backward village women. You're not a child anymore, Katrina. You're becoming a woman."

Katrina pulled the bedcovers down on her side. Last night, sleeping in the same bed with her mother had felt cramped and bad. Now, even though her mother called her grown up, she had the feeling she wanted to roll over against her mother and cuddle there like a little girl.

"I wanted to yell at those women in the village," she admitted, lying back on the pillow. "I wanted to yell at you too. But I didn't."

Her mother smiled. "I'm sure you'll soon find an opportunity."

Katrina searched the bedcovers for her mother's hand. Finding it, she held fast. "Remember you used to say to Daddy when he would yell, 'Please, Larry, be civilized.' Remember?"

"Yes."

"And then he yelled even worse. He said you were calling him a black ape, a primitive man. He said it was your subconscious bigotry against blacks coming out."

"Yes."

Katrina hesitated. "Do you hate him for what he did to your face?" The question came blurting out, and Katrina waited for the answer, butterflies startling her guts.

"I don't want to," Mama said. "But for a while I think I will hate him. I hate him for sleeping with other women. I hate him for hitting me." Tears came to her eyes, and she clamped Katrina's hand tightly.

"I'm sorry, Mama."

"I hate him for divorcing me too. I hate him for not getting on a plane and chasing me here."

She turned to Katrina, a tear dropping off her eye like a tiny runnel, whitening a line of Mama's tan skin in its watery transparency. "You're old enough to understand, Katrina, how a woman can have lots of feelings at once. I hate him, but I miss him. It is very confusing."

"Yes!" Katrina squeezed her mother's hand—this was the first thing she had understood clearly all day.

"And you know what? I think I am a bigot. I think I do believe blacks are inferior. I won't admit that to anyone but my daughter."

This shocked Katrina, for it made her think of herself and her blackness. But like an adult, she understood that her mother did not mean her. Her mother meant something else. This something else she couldn't clearly see.

Mama turned her head back to the ceiling, talking as if to the fan up there. "We can't get away from who we really are. Sometimes, I think it's as if our voices go down deep into old places. We awaken the people in there, we awaken the past. We revive it all. Pain revives it. The people of our own blood start to rise up, very slowly, and they bring their arms around us. We can't get away from them. What we can do is try to be our own safe little island, try not to lose our tempers like your father did, try not to hit and beat and hurt. We have to always be civilized. Even if I am bigoted, I will have dignity, I will be civilized. And I will not return to your father. He is not civilized. I do not respect him. Even though I still love him, in a strange way, I do not respect him."

Katrina tried to fully understand the difference between respect and love.

Her mother smiled, turning back, kissing her forehead. "I love you, Katrina, more than anything. We'll be fine now, the two of us. I'll write again. We'll do what we have to do."

Katrina saw in her mind's eye how her father had come up to her mother three days before, yelled at her, wheeled her around by the shoulders, then slapped her on the face. Katrina shivered at the memory and did not let go of her mother. Words started to form in her, something like, "I'll hate Papa too if you want," but she realized the childishness of them before they sang out her mouth. Instead, she whispered, "Mama, I will always be your friend."

Her mother looked into her eyes, and then melted. She began to sob. Katrina had not seen or felt emotion like this from Mama in years. Katrina held her mother like a sister, and she too cried to her mother's shoulder. How strong Mama always was, how quiet and strong. But now she spasmed with terrible pain.

"Mama," Katrina soothed. "We'll be okay, Mama." Katrina ran her hand on her mother's thick black hair, tracing a gray streak, then kissing her head through the blackness. A hair stuck to her lip, pulling slightly at her as it let go.

Katrina waited, her mother in her arms, for her mother to speak. Her own tears subsided, her head filling with images of the village, then her father back in India, then Jahiri. She felt sad, but she did not feel alone. This was the first time she had not felt alone in days.

As her tears subsided, Mama pulled her head away but not her arms. She looked into her daughter's eyes. Katrina saw that lamplight lit her mother's pupils, making them golden.

"I'm sorry I need you to be my friend," her mother said, sniffling, recovering. "I wish you could enjoy just being a girl. But you can't. You have to grow up fast. I'm sorry."

Katrina said, "that's alright," but truly did not know what to say.

"Will we see Papa again?" she asked, almost regretting it as her mother pulled away, her head back on her own pillow.

"I think it will be a very long time, Katrina."

"I think so too," Katrina said immediately, maturely, expecting to feel anger or sadness but instead, as if an equation had finally finished on the blackboard, feeling clear.

And she thought she understood something more of what her mother and Aunt Nura had been talking about at dinner, though she couldn't form it in words, except to say to her mother, "I'll try to act like a civilized person."

"I know you will," Mama said. "One day you may fly off with some man," she continued, staring into the air. "You'll leave your home—it seems it will be Egypt you leave, like I did. You'll throw out the whole civilized life for a new way of being, a new freedom, something really interesting, like America, so uncivilized, so exciting with new possibilities. It's always freedom we're looking for when we're young, especially if we've got a mind of our own. Like you do. Like I did. Nothing else matters but freedom.

"I hope when you go seeking it, you won't end up like you did tonight in that village. Or like I ended up, taking a man's drunken beatings. I want you to find a different freedom, Katrina.

"But no matter what, it is your dignity you will have to take forward into life, whether you find your sweet freedom or not. You will be civilized, not barbaric. When you're my age—when even the freedom shrivels and it's back to basics, it's flight and then survival—you'll have at least your dignity. Does this make sense to you, Katrina?"

Katrina had heard her mother talk about big things like this so many times, but she had never listened this way, with no thoughts of her own invading, just her mind open.

"I think so."

Her mother smiled at her, leaned over, and kissed her forehead. "Alright, then. Let's try to sleep. And let's try to be friends."

Mama turned the light off, and Katrina lay with her in the darkness. Katrina lay there long after her mother began to breathe evenly. She wanted to say things, ask things, hear things. Her head was filled with conversations and images, as if her life thus far was suddenly replaying itself. She remembered being a little girl in Jaipur sitting on a toilet and a snake coming up into the bowl. How she had screamed! She remembered her Ayah, a shriveled old woman who helped raise her. She remembered her family's *dhudhwalla*, a stooped man who tyrannized three laundry women with tongue lashings. She remembered the parasites that had burrowed into her skin after a monsoon season. She remembered the times her father had slapped her hard in the face.

As Katrina fell asleep that night, she lay in bed with her mother in Aswan, Egypt, not in India or America, and she did not know the end of either anger or fear—in fact, she thought she might just be at the beginning of what it meant to truly understand how terribly alone life could be—but she felt a strange stabbing of joy. Her mother, she thought, had shared with her a secret to life that could not have been shared in any other place, nor in any other way. Katrina expected to rise from bed tomorrow with a surly expression and a vast indifference to her mother's ideas, but for now, as she listened to Mama turn over in bed, a low moan emitting from her mouth, the soft hiss of bedcovers moving about her, Katrina reached to touch her mother's hair, and drifted off to sleep in the folds of her mother's breathing.

F